Knox Chase
on the Case
of the
Valentine's Day
Mystery

By

Adam Lipsius

Book Cover Artist, Matt Chase © 2016
Blurb Illustration by Amit Tayal

Uptown 6, LLC
Denver
Copyright © 2016, Adam Lipsius
All rights reserved.
ISBN: 978-0615988887

Advanced Reviews of *Knox Chase on the Case*

August 13th, 11 years ago.

"An utterly charming adventure brimming with wit, heart, and intrigue. A stellar debut!"
-- Ransom Riggs, <u>New York Times</u> Best Selling Author of <u>Ms. Peregrine's Home for Peculiar Children</u>

"Lipsius brings a black-and-white hero into the vibrant world of today's kids. Children, parents, and grandparents will find plenty to laugh about and bond over with this soon-to-be serial classic."
-- Brigid Pasulka, PEN/Hemingway Award Winning Author of <u>A Long Long Time Ago & Essentially True</u>

More Reviews of *Knox Chase on the Case*

"Move over Hardy Boys, there's a new set of detectives in town! Knox Chase and KC Green are on the case, and the bad guys had better beware. What happens when you combine a fictional, black and white gumshoe, with a modern elementary school kid? You get a rollicking page turner that is sure to find a massive audience."

"I thoroughly enjoyed the book! Congrats to Adam Lipsius for a literary triumph - an instant classic- that is sure to be a source of family bonding for years to come!"

-- Tom Mustin, CBS 4 News Denver Reporter

"Books like Knox Chase on the Case of The Valentine's Day Mystery are a treasure because they inspire young girls and boys to not only use their imagination but to also become aware of the many potential adventures they can follow as they make their journey through this experience called life. K.C. Green's story is told with good tongue-in-cheek humor and is fast-paced enough to hold a young audiences' attention. We can't wait for the next Knox Chase sequel!"

-- Dee Long, Amazon.com Reviewer

Dedication

Mommy Head, Hot Dot and Squiggle, if you hadn't grown my heart three whole sizes then the next three hundred pages would have been missing. I love you, and this is all your fault... *so THERE!!!*

Table of Contents

Chapter 1

THE NIGHT BEFORE EVERYTHING WENT COMPLETELY WRONG... WHEN STUFF JUST HAPPENED BADLY, IN A REGULAR SORT OF WAY...

"KC Green / Private Eye." The letters were brush-stroked into a circle on a second story window so you could read them from the small-town street below. They felt so professional, you couldn't tell they'd been hand painted by an even smaller boy. KC Green did it the evening his family moved in to their old new house on the best worst day he'd ever had. All these years later, he still hadn't gotten a single client from stenciling his name backwards on the glass, but his sign had brought him a lot more business than he'd bargained for.

It was past one in the morning on the night before Valentine's Day, and those words were projected from the light of a lamp post down below. They hovered on the ceiling over the sleeping investigator's head in a shadowy bulls-eye, framed by the bannisters of his old wooden bed. Everything seemed quiet, except KC shook uneasily in pajamas that barely still fit from his eighth birthday. He was almost twelve now.

Yellow-white light reflected off of his ceiling and washed over the young detective's cluttered bedroom. In its glow, the tousled, brown haired boy didn't look funny or funny peculiar. He looked handsome -- old ladies always told him how good-looking he was, and when his eyes were open, they were big and brown and smiling almost all the time.

His room resembled an old-fashioned movie-set filled with film noir touches. He had his Dad's original Knox Chase on the Case books on oak shelves. There was a mission-style wooden desk with a shaded green lamp turned down low and a brass stand for a fifty-four inch gumshoe's trench coat.

Surrounded by his vintage treasures, the reflected glare didn't shine light on anything other than a 6th grader sleeping uneasily. As he rolled over into shadow and tucked into a little ball, though, KC's face furrowed like he expected something.

"Pssst...," hissed the voice of someone who wasn't there. "Pal...., KC."

A tall man who could pass for a silent film star appeared in the room, but not through any door. Instead, he just flickered into being, as if pure light had whirred into human form out of some black and white movie. One second there was nothing, and the next instant this old fashioned detective from a pulp fiction magazine was towering over KC's bed.

He had a weathery face that was always 5 o'clock and bearded stubble no razor had ever really shaved. Sepia-toned, like photos of somebody's great grandfather after some war, he wore a trench coat and fedora hat covering up a full head of hair, a rumpled suit and other peoples' secrets.

Black and white and gray, like granite, he was both there and not there at the same time. Illuminated somehow, he seemed to pop and brighten and sputter, but there was no movie projector playing anywhere. It was like he'd walked off the set of his last film and into the present day in search of a new script to play.

This was no ordinary person. It was Knox Chase, the hero of hundreds of unsolvable mysteries, and he fidgeted, impatient to get back on the case.

"To sleep perchance to dream, my friend, but the rub is you gotta wake up. Right now." Knox drew two fingers to his lips and horse-whistled.

"Knox!" KC hugged his mattress tighter, pleading "I don't want to play chess, I was..."

"You don't care about a case, that's your business. But I don't take responsibility so lightly," Knox intoned.

KC opened one eye a tiny sliver and turned to ask, "What case?"

"Even when you're not on a case, you're on a case. Entiende?"

"No," KC groaned, and his one eye rolled closed.

Knox lectured him, "Bad guys don't sleep - not literally, of course - everybody sleeps--"

"Not you," KC surrendered, "and not me when you're around." He swung his feet over, slouched up and heaved himself out of bed, "Why are you here right now?"

"A funny feeling that something isn't right," Knox said, watching KC don his fedora from the bedpost and snatch a contraption from the desk. "All a private eye has is his instincts. At best a clue points due North, but it's your job to find the trail. And that's instinct."

KC chuckled as he unfurled his tin can monoscope into a full-length spy device. He shook his head and scanned the small-town's quiet streets.

His Dad had started reading Knox's pearls of wisdom to him back when he was still in his mom's womb. The real-life detective had shown up to finish his 'education' as soon as his family got to Cornelia. Only, with Knox teaching him, KC felt like graduation was not in the plans. The pulp fiction anti-hero of sixteen novels, four movies and hundreds of comic books had never once been at a loss for lessons, and since he was stuck following around a kid in the middle of nowhere, Knox's biggest trouble was there was never enough trouble.

"Do you see it, yet?" Knox asked, betraying the grin he was feeling within.

KC looked harder. He scanned the houses across the street. Through the looking glass he'd soldered together with thick lenses and soup and sauce cans, he poured over the neighborhood inch by inch. By lucky coincidence, he finally caught a flash of something white in a tree in Memorial Square.

"What is that?" KC asked, focusing on the branches around the flashing foot but seeing nothing more than leaves shaking.

He could have sworn it was a sneaker... in a tree... in the center of town. But why would that be there?

"There's one way to know something, and I mean know it..." Knox began.

"You mean besides you just telling me," KC yawned.

Knox never just told KC what he knew. You think anybody gave me a hand-out when I was starting-out, kid? Sure! With a balled up fist...

"To find out for yourself," Knox winked.

KC sighed and looked at the rumpled sheets he might not see again that night. He pulled on sweat pants over his pajamas and slipped into a pair of high-tops parked at the base of his bed.

"Pavement, greet our feet," Knox declared as he flickered out.

It was like the film frames on a movie screen whirring to a stop.

KC laced up his shoes, muttering, "If you even have feet..."

"I heard that," Knox echoed invisibly.

KC rolled his eyes, grabbed his cell phone from the counter, slid the monoscope into his backpack and put his trench coat on from the rack. Then he snuck out the door.

Chapter 2

Outside, jogging down the street to his rendezvous with a stranger in a tree, frozen breaths hovered behind KC like icy thought bubbles. He figured the perp was peering inside an unsuspecting guest's room at the Grand View Hotel. The joint was called the *Grand View* because there was a VFW statue that was pretty to look at, *but being the view probably wasn't what the hotel's guests had in mind.*

KC thought his options over. He wouldn't call Cornelia PD 'Detective' Grist, the town's resident investigator because that guy couldn't find his way out of a paper bag if he fell inside looking for the last cruller. When a bunch of houses were broken into the year before and Grist assumed it was workers passing through who must have done it, KC set up a nanny-cam stake-out that uncovered the actual burglar's license plate. Since then, Grist had hated him.

KC did pull out his cell phone, though, and Knox Chase whirred to life beside him. "I don't trust those things, KC, and I trust the slobs on the other end of them even less."

"I'm calling my father," KC warned him.

"Case closed," Knox smirked.

He didn't like KC's dad. Ron Green was a Special Agent for the FBI, and maybe since Knox was a private eye from the bad old days, when government agents could out-tough the criminals they were after, he didn't believe the Feds were on the level. KC thought Knox was just being mean, though.

"I don't see anybody lining up to take care of you, KC, so it must be your job, and there's no time like the present to get cracking," Knox advised in a dead-pan which was as passionate as the gumshoe ever seemed to get.

"You want me to take this guy down out of that tree on my own? Are you crazy?" KC huffed, but Knox was already shaking his head.

"No...! Get the lay of the land first. See what kind of no-good he's up to. *Then* you follow this bright boy home and peek a look through his belongings later... when he's out misadventuring. That's what I'd do."

KC looked at him, mouth open in disbelief. It was late, and he had school in the morning, and he still hadn't written his card for Cat. To say she was the girl he liked would be like saying New York has... buildings. Or sunrise is... colorful. You wouldn't be wrong, exactly, but you'd miss the scope and grandeur of the thing, completely.

KC had like-liked Cat since the moment she showed up in town a year after he did, and he had like-liked her for so long and so deeply there weren't enough words to get the point across. In fact, he like-liked her so much, KC had trouble even opening his mouth in front of her, because so many notions struck him at the same time that they all crammed into each other behind his gums.

Every time his tongue tried to get some fraction of this point across, he was worse than speechless. His pupils dilated, his pulse raced, and his jaw just jangled open and shut producing nothing but heavy breaths and hot embarrassment. On the rare occasions when he pried his lips wide enough apart for an entire word to blurt out, he'd shout something like *nice...!* or *pretty....!* and then be too horrified to continue, cheeks flushing red.

It was the pressure of what he had inside his head building up and shooting out, but he couldn't explain that when everyone looked at him like he was a lunatic. Everyone except Cat, that is. She'd just smile sweetly, but he knew she had to think he was a moron and was just too nice to say.

Now Knox wanted him to camp out on the night before Valentine's Day behind a tree waiting to see if some guy did something creepy?! *Valentine's is the one day a year where you're supposed to show people how you feel about them.* This was KC's chance, and he wasn't going to blow it staying out til sunrise in the freezing cold. He brought the phone to his ear.

Knox took one last swipe at KC's dad, though, "Your Old Man's a G-man who can't even catch a bad guy after three years of tailing him. How's he gonna help from a thousand miles away?"

KC glared at Knox and hit the call button.

It wasn't KC's dad's fault that this master jewel thief he was trying to catch still wasn't behind bars. Ron Green was one of the best undercover agents the bureau had ever had, and this was his first case after putting an entire crime syndicate out of business. He'd been promoted to special agent and given his own team and a super hard case to work, and after three years of investigating, he still didn't even know what this mastermind's name was. Just his initials. BS. Mr. BS.

"Send him my regards, why don'cha," Knox scoffed.

"Yeah. Right." KC stopped jogging long enough to catch his breath while waiting for his dad to pick-up. The phone pulsed in his ear.

Ron answered his end of the line, and he sounded worried, surprised and annoyed at the same time. "Is everything okay? What are you doing up, KC? Do you know what time it is?"

Maybe it wasn't such a good idea calling his dad.

"I'm fine--" was all KC could say before his father cut him off.

"I'm interviewing a person of interest, so you better have a good reason for being up."

KC smiled as he whispered into the phone, "I'm in Memorial Square across from the old Grand View Hotel. There's a perp--"

KC's dad shout-whispered into the phone, "You're out of the house again?!"

Knox smirked a little beside him as KC answered, "Yeah, and I was hoping you could phone it into Cornelia PD. They don't really take my calls anymore. It's a 15-37, and the guy's up a tree--."

Knox interrupted, "You haven't actually found out what this citizen is doing up there, which is why I wanted *us* to investigate."

Covering the phone, KC responded, "I can use my imagination."

Then he whispered, "Thanks, Dad," hanging up the line just as Ron Green started to scream, "You're out of bed tracking down a--."

KC crouched low beside the corner of a building as Knox advised him, "You'd better turn that squawk box off before you spook the looker."

"Oh, yeah," KC said and shut his phone down.

"Now sit tight while we wait for the cavalry. That's why they get paid the big bucks," Knox advised, but KC frowned as he peered through his monoscope at the figure in the tree.

The branches were shaking like mad, and all he could make out was a sweat suit and those bright white sneakers.

"Then what'd you wake me up for if we weren't going to put a stop to it?" KC demanded.

"Most of anything in life is just showing up," Knox expounded. "Pay attention, and you're bound to figure out the mysteries of the universe. Who did what to whom... and why... and how. Keep your nose out of too many scrapes and you'll learn a thing or two, but sometimes you poke the hive just to hear how the bees hum. I wouldn't have called those yahoos if it was me, but you turned to the boys in blue. So now I say, let the chips fall where they may."

"The chips," KC repeated, as a grin spread across his lips. He had an idea.

KC raced low across the street to crouch behind a near-by bush with Knox Chase jogging up-right beside him, asking "What are you gonna do, look him down?"

KC chuckled back, "I'm gonna scare him down."

He said it loud enough to make the tree branches stop shaking, but KC picked up a handful of wood chips and smiled at Knox like this was the best idea he'd ever had. The seasoned private eye shook his head, grimacing, but there was no stopping KC as he filled the pockets of his trench coat. He palmed one especially good-sized hunk from the pile and lobbed it high in the air towards the tree.

It landed above this peeper's head and clunked its way noisily to the ground.

"Hunh," a startled voice grunted.

"That'll get his attention," KC whispered.

Knox frowned, not so impressed. "Have you actually thought about what you'd do if this guy fell out of his tree? Or, heaven forefend, climbed down to get your attention?"

Instead of answering, KC chucked another wood chip.

"Who's there?" a startled voice rang out from high up.

KC grinned like he'd just invented gravity and then scurried off to another hiding place on the other side of the tree.

Knox watched him go as the voice in the tree murmured, "It's all-right, Petunia," in a soothing voice.

"Petunia?" Knox wondered out loud, before fading out from his previous position and projecting himself right beside his 11-year old protégé again.

"It isn't the next move or the next move after that," Knox lectured KC in his new spot. "It's 23 moves to check-mate, my friend, and that's if you lay the right traps and peer around enough corners. You're just making it up as you go along..."

"Knox, you're driving me nuts!" KC hissed just a little too loudly.

"I hear you!" answered the voice from the tree. "Who's Knox? Who are you?"

KC frowned at his friend like this was his fault for egging him on, and he deepened his voice as much as he could before shouting "Climb down outta that tree, punk. We got you surrounded!"

Then he let loose a whole handful of wood chips that rained down upon the stranger in the tree.

"Ugh, Aught!" the man shrieked back from the end of a long branch. Beside him a kitten meowed, and the man said, "No, Petunia, daddy's coming."

Knox shrugged a *got me* back at KC, who's smile had collapsed into a worried frown. He ran warily up beneath the tree and looked up to see an older man clinging wobbly to the thin arm of the maple.

"Mr. Jenkins?" KC gasped, "Is that you?"

Mr. Jenkins ran the Antiques Boutique on Main Street. He was fussy and opposed to children on principle, but KC knew it wasn't likely he was leering into hotel room windows or plotting a robbery.

"The Green boy. I should have known, and to whom were you speaking?" Mr. Jenkins demanded, voice trembling, legs wrapped around the shaky branch which creaked eerily as it dipped beneath his weight.

Six inches past his grasping fingers, a white kitten purred and pawed her foot, ready to jump.

"Petunia, don't!" Mr. Jenkins hollered too late, because the fluffy puff ball had already leaped, yowling the fifteen feet towards the ground.

KC breathed in deep, twisted and stuck his arms out in the same direction the kitten was plummeting. It was a miracle. He'd never caught a baseball or a dodge ball or a cold before, but he threw himself at just the right instant, and Petunia landed contentedly in the palms of his hands. Licking his skin with her sandpaper tongue, she strolled onto the grass as KC laughed. Relieved.

"Don't let her get away, strange boy!" Mr. Jenkins shouted above him, and KC scrambled to his feet to scoop up Petunia again.

That's when Mr. Jenkins' branch snapped loudly in two with him on the wrong end. He yelled as he fell, toppling five yards to the grass beneath and thudding on his back precisely where KC had just been.

The antiques man didn't look dead, but his face was turning purple as his eyes bulged out and his lips locked in a funny position. He wheezed to breathe, but with all the wind knocked out of him, no air could get in.

KC's mouth dropped open, and his head swiveled in every direction until he saw red and blue police lights approach from the distance. *Thank you, Dad!* was all he could think, and he turned back to Mr. Jenkins to reassure him. Before he could say anything to the not-breathing man, though, Petunia hopped out of his hands and plopped onto Mr. Jenkins' belly. The weight of the kitty made him cough and sputter, but mostly normal breaths wheezed in and out of his gaping mouth again.

His skin went back to pink as he heaved the words "Thank you HUNHhhh for catching HUNHhhh Petunia..."

Knox turned up beside KC just then and said "He may not have been a cat burglar, but at least you caught his kitty."

Chapter 3

VALENTINE'S DAY, AKA, THE DAY EVERYONE IN
SCHOOL BECAME CONVINCED KC WASN'T JUST A
WEIRDO... BUT ALSO A MENACE...

KC sat on the edge of his bed with a clipboard in his lap, nibbling a pencil. It was 7:45 in the morning. His electric clock churned, and the sun burned his neck through the window, but his brain wouldn't work. He was running out of time to dream up a Valentine for Cat.

He hadn't gotten back to bed until 3 am the night before, and when the alarm rang three hours later it felt like a car was running over his brain then backing up to squish it all over again. His mom had warned him that they'd talk about his punishment for sneaking out this morning, so he had to work fast on his card. The last thing he wanted to do was tell her about Cat, but absolutely nothing was coming to him.

He crumpled up a sheet of KC Green / Private Eye letter-head with another useless attempt scribbled across it and tossed it in the garbage bin on top of two dozen other balled-up false starts. He grabbed a fresh piece of paper from a wire basket on his desk and breathed deep.

Again and again. Faster and faster. Staring at the empty page beneath his logo made him hyperventilate.

Somehow he was supposed to compose something that would explain how much he liked Cat without creeping her out, but it wasn't much easier talking to the page than it was saying how he felt to the real girl, herself. In person. His fingers got tongue-tied just thinking about it.

Beside him, his best friend Benjy Young sat at KC's desk, leaning in close to read something on the computer. He kept shaking his head and chuckling.

Benjy was taller than KC and Chinese, but his whole family had been in Cornelia since his great-great-grandfather worked on the Transcontinental Railroad after the Civil War. There was even a picture of this guy personally laying the last track at Promontory Point when the whole country was connected by train. According to Benjy, this made KC a 'misplaced New Yorker,' which was fine with him.

Knox Chase watched them from the corner, sucking a lollipop, not that Benjy noticed. Benjy had never seen the real-life, black-and-white detective, even though KC had made him read all of his books in hopes he might.

KC jotted something down on the paper in front of him.

"'Cat, words fail me when I look in your eyes...?' Sound like a good start?" he asked Benjy.

"Incredible," Benjy answered without listening.

KC looked over and saw a picture of himself splayed across the front page of the *Cornelia Courant's* online version. In the photo, KC had his hand out to try and block his face from the camera, and his other hand was being pulled by his clearly exasperated mother. The caption under the photo read, "'Loathe the boy, I might, but he saved Petunia,' Gerald Jenkins explained why he wasn't pressing charges."

Benjy puckered, "Now I know why my mom wouldn't let me walk to school with you today." Then he turned back to the article to read it aloud, "Cornelia's 11-year old crime-fighter, KC Green, nearly cost Gerald Jenkins more than his pet pussy-cat in his latest misadventure."

"I'm almost 12," KC muttered under his breath. Then he caught sight of Knox grinning in the corner, and he snapped, "What are you smiling at?"

"I'm not smiling, KC." Benjy stared at his friend like he was playing with a 51-card deck. "You made the front page. You're infamous."

KC crumpled up his latest piece of paper and threw it in Benjy's face. "I thought you came over here to help me with this Valentine."

"I tried, but you said there was no talking you out of it."

"Come on! This is how my Dad asked my Mom out...," KC insisted.

Benjy broke it to KC, "Yeah... After he saved her from a hold-up. You've never even held a door for Cat. You can't string three words together in front of her."

"All-right...," KC gave up, putting his pencil down. He knew it was hopeless. "But don't you think she's amazing?" He wanted to be talked into trying it anyway.

It wasn't just that Cat was pretty. She was undeniably pretty. She was just so, so, real. All the other girls giggled about things he couldn't even understand and had no idea what they were talking about. Cat would just sigh, not to be mean, but she'd sigh because she didn't want to talk about clothes or say jerky things about other kids or wax on about some new singer.

And Cat could sing! She had this voice that was soulful and deep and throaty and full, and she played piano, too. Her mom was from South America and was some kind of a musical genius, and evidently Cat was even better.

She wasn't allowed to play volleyball or basketball or anything where she might break her hands and mess up her piano playing. Her mom had complained to the school about it after Cat's first day, but Cat never said a word.

She was so good at piano that Mr. Ringmeyer even let her accompany him back when she was a first grader. He said it was so he could keep an eye on the boys who were going to goof around and mess up chorus rehearsal, but even then she could play things without looking at the music. Just after hearing them a few times.

KC used to watch her with his mouth open and sometimes got yelled at because he'd forget to sing. He'd just stand there listening. In a room full of twenty-two other people, it was like it was just her and him.

"It's just... Cat's cool. Smart. Talented. And when the light hits her hair..."

Benjy leapt out of his chair waving a copy of <u>Knox Chase on the Case of the Homicidal Heartbreak</u> in KC's face. "Ask yourself what the real Knox Chase would do. Don't you read? Love's for suckers!"

"And saps..." Knox Chase smirked.

"You're incapable of love and bitter about it!" KC cut Knox off.

"What makes you say I'm incapable of love?" Benjy frowned.

"That's low, my friend," Knox added.

"Nothing. Sorry, Benjy. But I'm writing this poem, so you can either help or hit the bricks..." KC apologized to Benjy while letting Knox know he meant business.

"All-right, but you're really sensitive today," Benjy sulked back down at the computer to search for romantic poetry.

KC's door opened and his mom leaned in. She was pretty with reddish-brown hair, a doll's complexion and blue eyes that used to laugh like KC's still did. She frowned at him before noticing Benjy sitting there. That made her smile.

"KC, we need to-- Oh, hi Benjy. What are you two up to?"

"We're--" Benjy started to say, but KC interrupted him, "We're working, and we would appreciate some privacy."

Benjy would have told her everything, because that's how he rolled, and KC didn't need his mother inquiring about his love-life or his like-life or his life-life for that matter.

She frowned again, "All-right, Bud, but you and I have a date to discuss your punishment."

"You mean my punishment for being there to help Mr. Jenkins after he fell out of that tree?" KC asked with a straight face.

"Maybe for helping Mr. Jenkins actually fall out of the tree..." Benjy muttered to himself, making Mary Green laugh.

"How about for sneaking out of the house? Again? For the umpteenth time?" She warned KC while suppressing a grin.

"Okay, so is you sticking around while I'm trying to do something with my friend going to count as part of my punishment?" KC pressed.

Benjy gaped at him, but his mom just sighed and shook her head.

"No, KC. You haven't been *that* bad, but keep pushing me, and I might just move into this office of yours, and you'll be sleeping on the floor until college. You hear me?"

KC nodded and whispered, "Thanks, Mom."

"We'll finish up later," she told him and then turned back to Benjy and said, "How's your mom?"

"Worried," Benjy answered, looking back over at KC.

Before Mary Green could ask what Benjy meant, though, KC said "Thanks, Mom!"

"All-right..." she muttered, backing away and shutting the door behind her.

"That's no way to speak to a lady," Knox stood up and tossed his lollipop towards the garbage bin, though the candy flickered out of existence before crossing the rim.

Benjy also got up to go, "I'd better get back before my Mom finds out I'm here."

"Fine. Abandon me. I'm terrible at this," KC lay back against his mattress.

Knox shook his head, but pity warmed his frown a little as he asked, "Help is a four-letter word, my friend. You sure you want to ask for it?"

KC nodded without Benjy noticing.

"Depending on people becomes habit-forming. This is a one-time thing. Comprende?" Knox warned.

KC nodded again that he understood and grinned eagerly as Knox warmed to his subject "Then try this, compadre, and don't blame me when it works. 'Cat, you take my breath away...'"

"Cat you take my breath away?" KC repeated.

Benjy heard him and stopped packing up his things, shrugging "Not bad..."

KC smiled and picked up his clipboard.

"One look in your eyes, and I realize what I'm missing," Knox said.

KC repeated the line in a mutter as he etched it on the paper.

Benjy marveled, "KC, you're a poet?"

"He could be if he used those books I recommended for something other than door-stops and coasters," Knox complained.

KC cleared his throat, and the detective obliged, "My heart falters a beat, knowing it's not mine to keep."

Reading over KC's shoulder, Benjy questioned the use of the word falter, but KC kept on scribbling.

"But the gift I long to give, a heart-felt sign..." KC said as he wrote Knox's beautiful lines.

Then as KC finished the poem and drew a heart around the verses, Benjy read the last bit out-loud, "'Cat, will you be my Valentine?'" He thought it over, scrunching his face as he re-read the poem again before declaring, "I don't want to throw up. It's a miracle! I'll see you later."

That reminded KC, "Your mom really wouldn't let you walk to school with me?"

Benjy shrugged and slung his backpack over his shoulder.

When they were little, Benjy's mom wanted them to hang out all the time. They'd hunt for 'clues' in the attic and solve 'mysteries' all over town. She was the county comptroller and probably liked the idea that KC's dad worked for the FBI. Lately, though, as KC's 'investigations' had gotten a little bad publicity and he'd ticked off Detective Grist she didn't seem as keen on the idea.

KC swallowed. His Adam's Apple was suddenly the size of a grapefruit, but he had his Valentine for Cat which he slid into a manila envelope as he grinned at Knox.

"You're welcome, Romeo."

Chapter 4

Hearts hung from all the lamp-posts and store windows in downtown Cornelia like a giant baker had frosted whatever his cake squirter could reach. There were fat baby angels, paper chains and pink bunting adorning almost everything, and KC and Knox marched past it in their matching outfits. The folks alongside them, though, only saw an oddly dressed boy walking somewhere, all alone. An older woman even walked through Knox without either of them breaking stride.

KC clutched the manila envelope with his poem inside. All-right, it was the poem Knox had written for KC to pass off as his own creation. His stomach was gurgling, but not because of Cat. KC couldn't stop thinking about Benjy and his mom.

Does she really think I'm a bad influence? Does Benjy think I'm going nuts, too? AM I crazy for talking to Knox?

They were approaching the Antique Boutique, and KC muttered out the side of his mouth so no one would think he was talking to himself, "I hope Mr. Jenkins is okay."

Knox grumbled back, "Kids are like radios built without an off-switch. Nothing to do but wait out the batteries..."

"What are you talking about?" KC snapped, attracting nervous stares from folks walking past.

"You thought you were helping last night, sure. But if you let your head do the thinking maybe you woulda learned something instead."

KC stared back at Knox, puzzled, so he spelled it out, "You have three friends in this world: here, here and here," Knox pointed to his brain and then held up each fist. Then he tapped his chest, "Smart and heart rhyme kid, but that has nothing to do with it."

KC hadn't banked on a lecture this early. His fragile brain was already straining to deal with today's problems instead of rehashing those from the night before.

"You know why I took you out last night?" Knox asked, and KC shook his head and gritted his teeth. "Because this town is a jigsaw puzzle, and we haven't got all the pieces, yet."

KC looked up and breathed. He sniffled back a throat full of resentment, and he breathed. He blinked his eyes clear, staring fixedly at Knox, and he breathed, because it took all his concentration on what his friend was saying to keep his feelings from getting in the way.

"You like putting things together. Building things. That's swell, but-- Look Out!" Knox hollered, but it was too late.

KC walked full-steam ahead into somebody backing onto the sidewalk from behind Mr. Jenkins' building. It was a tall stranger in dark blue coveralls and sun-glasses and a baseball hat and beard.

The guy flopped over weirdly, toppling to the ground on his hands and knees as he tossed a manila envelope into the air. It was identical to the one KC had been holding until he lost his grip in the collision. The two letters flipped and shuffled a couple of times before landing on top of one another on the sidewalk.

KC reached for the pile. "I'm sorry, I should have--," but he stopped short, struck by the stranger's small hands which were doing the same thing.

There was a hoodie over this guy's head and big mirrored shades blocking his gaze. He simply grunted and scooped up the top envelope in a bandana he'd already been holding. KC stared a moment too long as this stranger wobbled up off of his knees and puffed into the distance like he was wrestling an imaginary breeze.

"Weird," KC said before getting back up.

"I'll say," Knox insisted. "Let's follow him."

"No! I've got something more important to do." KC was thinking that he'd already made the front page once this week.

People walking past looked at him again as he was apparently talking to himself, but Knox couldn't care less. "In the old days, I'd have followed that guy into whatever gin joint or back-alley he bounced into. But now you're letting him get away?"

KC nodded "Unh Hunh" and stood up as he set off for school in the opposite direction.

"This is finally our chance," Knox implored, but KC ignored him and kept walking.

"Then you just tiptoe through the mine-field of young love solo, friend!" Knox hollered.

KC raised a hand in a backward wave and marched off. He didn't watch as Knox Chase shook his head in disapproval and turned to follow the stranger.

≈≈≈≈≈≈≈≈≈

KC walked into the classroom alone. He could feel his cheeks burning red from so much blood pumping there was nowhere else for it to go, not unless he exploded. He pushed the door open a little too hard. It thudded into the back-stop, and heads looked up.

KC's heart jack-hammered in his throat now, threatening to choke him.

Across the room, Benjy smiled, trying hard not to crack up. His eyes rolled, then he jerked his head over in the direction of Cat's table. KC looked.

Around her, all the girls in the class were buzzing as they opened pink and red and white envelopes and read each others' notes. KC's mind raced as he tried to swallow a glob of fear. *She wouldn't show MY card to her friends*, he asked himself, *would she?*

Asking for help didn't come easily to KC, but nevertheless, he gritted his teeth and looked up into the ceiling tiles and very quietly, very discretely, his lips barely moving, he said, "Knox, hey Knox!"

No answer. He kept peering up, waiting, unaware that a bigger kid named Bobby G was bearing down on him. The G stood for Grist because his dad was the same Detective Charlie Grist who detested KC. If it was possible, though, Bobby hated him even more. He'd gone from generally abusing him to specifically trying to kill him around the same time his dad started spreading the word that KC was no good.

KC didn't see Bobby's elbow cramming into the vulnerable part of his head, just behind his ear. All he saw were the black and white fireworks that ignited behind his eyelids when that sharp bone popped him good. It took KC a second to shake his brain clear.

Bobby hooted like a gorilla in the zoo, "You praying somebody bought you a Valentine, loser?"

He walked over to his tiny circle of dimly lit bulbs, and of course, it drew looks from everyone else in class. KC rubbed the sore spot and glanced over to Cat who knit her brows and smiled sympathetically. *Great, she thinks I'm a charity case.*

That's the moment Knox chose to answer his prayer by saying in thin air, "Here's some advice, sit down and forget the whole thing. Really."

KC shook his head, annoyed, and he said to no one in particular, "Thanks for nothing."

"Don't mention it," Bobby G answered, making his cronies laugh some more.

Then the bell rang, and KC gulped. It was like he was stuck inside a fish bowl. He was supposed to take his seat, and he was still holding his envelope in both hands, frozen.

He looked across the room into Cat's beautiful brown eyes, and he panted for a second, and everything felt like it was in slow motion. Like KC was trapped in a mound of jello and couldn't fight his way out.

Kids around him were murmuring, embarrassed for him.

Mrs. Pepper, the teacher, said, "That's enough, class," but to KC it sounded like "Ttthhaaaatt'sss Eeeeeennnoouuufffggh..."

He mustered every ounce of courage to walk over to Cat's table, feeling like he'd drop dead of a heart attack before he got there, but she smiled up at him and KC blushed.

"KC, is that for me?" she asked, and he was thankful that he could just nod his reply without having to open his mouth. He was afraid he'd throw up.

Cat opened the envelope, and then the smile in her eyes went out, smothered by worry. She lowered the paper to ask him a question, and the first thing he noticed was that his poem was gone. Instead of the card with the heart-shaped drawing and the words he'd been wanting to share since he'd met her five years earlier, there was a page of cut-out letters from a bunch of magazines. It looked like a ransom note.

He'd just started reading it upside down, G-I-V-E M-E T-H-- when her voice cut in, accusing him of something, "I don't understand?!"

Shaking his head, stammering, KC tried to say that neither did he, but Lorrie Haudi, the nosiest person ever born, snatched the paper out of Cat's hands and read the thing out loud, "'Give me the Piggy, and no one gets hurt?!'" She practically shouted it.

Faces went white, and Mrs. Pepper shot up out of her seat as Lorrie went on, "'Tick Tock Tick Tock?!?' OH NO!!! He's got a...." and she couldn't bring herself to say the word.

Instead she mouthed 'BOMB,' breathlessly, and all the kids in class froze, staring at him. Even Benjy shook his head, worried, and Bobby G grinned like he'd swallowed a canary. Cat glared at KC, and he couldn't find a word to say in his own defense, silently pleading with her to believe him.

"Stay calm, class. Let's evacuate two by two," Mrs. Pepper announced as brightly as she could, jogging over to the fire alarm by the door.

She pulled the red lever, and a claxon jolted everyone to action. Chairs scraped linoleum all over the school as kids scrambled out of their seats, mostly laughing. In their room, though, it was chaos as his classmates hurried for the door. Lorrie disappeared to the back of the class, and Cat stood up resentfully, burning with anger. She crumpled up the letter and dropped it at KC's feet before turning to go.

He wanted to follow her, but it was all he could do to say, "That's not my note. I didn't--,"

His mumbled protest didn't register over the throbbing alarm, though, and before he could move Lorrie Haudi stuffed something furry and scratchy into his hands. "Take the guinea pig, and leave us alone!" she sobbed before turning and bolting past Cat out the door.

KC looked down and found Salty, the class pet, in his palms. Lorrie must have run to his cage and pulled him out.

Chapter 5

TRUTH AND CONSEQUENCES...

"It wasn't my note!" KC was shouting for what felt like the millionth time.

He was sitting in the almost empty classroom, but the alarm had stopped ringing a long time ago. In front of him, Charlie Grist paced back and forth like it was Christmas Eve, and he couldn't wait to open the best present ever. The Cornelia Detective wore a bushy mustache and a shiny brown suit with his hand hitched on his hip to push open his jacket. It revealed the badge he'd fastened to his belt, and it felt to KC like maybe he'd practiced this move in the mirror.

Something glimmered over KC's shoulder, and he glanced up to see Knox Chase who commiserated, "You look pretty as a picture waiting to be framed. Don't tell this flat foot anything."

KC nodded, glad Knox was there, even if he was doling out the worst advice ever.

"Oh, that's right. The mysterious 'stranger' wrote the note," Grist made quote-fingers and leaned inches from KC's face to whisper "How stupid do you think I am?"

"He doesn't really want you to answer," Knox dead-panned.

KC burst out laughing, and he even dribbled a little spittle in Grist's face by accident. It was definitely the nerves.

"Sorry..."

"You think this is funny?" Grist wiped his hands across his moustache and forehead.

"No, I'm sorry. I just...," KC sputtered before picking up a pencil to sketch the stranger on the paper in front of him. "Let me show you who it was."

Grist sniffed skeptically, but KC's pencil carved an image on the page almost immediately. He started with the oval face and the weak chin covered in stubble, then drew in the over-sized glasses with mirrored frames and conjured tufts of hair poking from under the brim of a baseball hat.

"This is the guy who bumped into me on my way to school today," KC said while his pencil danced, eyes racing over the page. "6 feet tall, scruffy facial hair - not quite a beard. Dark blue hat and sunglasses. His hands, his manner weren't... right somehow. He wore a dark blue kind of uniform with a name tag, but I didn't catch the name."

Knox bristled, but KC ignored him and went on. "We knocked each other down, and he switched notes with me, I think by accident."

"You're full of accidents aren't you? Just like last night..."

KC literally bit his tongue to keep from talking back. Grist had spent the night before trying to persuade Mr. Jenkins to press charges against him. KC tasted blood in his mouth and had a tear in his eye, but he was going to finish this picture to show Grist who was *actually* up to something in Cornelia.

He held up the drawing of the stranger, and it was perfect. "Done," KC said, nursing his tongue against his lower gum so it sounded like *ton*.

The detective snatched the picture out of KC's hand and waved it around sarcastically, "How remarkable! I'll put out an APB for this guy right away. That stands for All Points Bulletin, by the way."

Grist dropped the page on the ground and glared down at KC like he was a big time perpetrator. "Forgive me if I'm not impressed with your powers of imagination, but I'm investigating a disturbance right here. Not in never-land. And I already know who did it."

"This copper has all the curiosity of a baloney on rye," Knox mused.

"That's the guy who wrote the note, *Detective*. He's the one you need to talk to."

KC put extra emphasis on the detective part since everyone knew the only reason Grist was 'Chief

Detective' -- and the only detective in Cornelia -- was because Chief Williamson felt bad for him. Grist's wife left him a few months ago, and this promotion was intended to restore his confidence. In KC's opinion, it had worked too well. Besides, Grist still did speed-trap duty like the other seven town policemen. Just now he got to wear a suit instead of a uniform. *Big deal!*

"Looking for trouble is my job," Grist glowered at KC. "And YOU. Are Trouble."

The two of them stared at each other, but KC didn't blink. "Is that what you're looking for, asleep in the patrol car on Highway 5 when you're supposed to be on duty?"

Knox smiled, but Grist poked KC in the chest and whispered, "I've got a cell in juvenile already picked out for you, punk! And I don't care who your father thinks he is, I'll sh--" but he cut himself off, mid-syllable, when the door opened behind him.

Will Worth, the school janitor, walked in. He looked exactly like the suspect KC had drawn and even wore the same dark blue coveralls. Brown hair, scruffy beard, handsome and over 6 feet tall, but he stooped from pushing a broom all day long.

KC did a double-take, and Knox nodded like he knew it all along. The resemblance even clicked for Grist who picked up KC's drawing from the floor and walked beside Will to hold it up next to his face. The janitor's jaw twitched, standing there, not daring to complain while Grist's eyes flicked back and forth.

Will did sneak a peek at KC, and he smiled when their eyes met. This didn't make sense.

He *could* have been the same guy, except Will had big hands. Also, the stranger had been knocked over by someone four and a half feet tall. Will seemed too solid for KC to make a dent in him. *And why would he come in here with a policeman in the room if he thought I might recognize him?*

"Will Worth... what are you doing here?" Grist finally asked as if rolling up a welcome mat to club him on the head with it.

"My broom and some of my things were missing, and--" Will began, but Grist talked right over him.

"Staying out of trouble?"

"Yes, sir."

Grist squinted at Will, dead-eye, until the janitor's shoulders sagged even lower. It was as if he was shrinking beneath the lawman's glare. Then the door opened again, and KC's mom poured into the room like a shaken bottle of soda.

"KC, are you all-right?" she dashed over to him.

Knox played an imaginary bugle to call in the cavalry.

"I'm fine, mom. Detective Grist was just showing me his new badge."

She and KC exchanged a look, and she turned on Grist, "Charlie, were you interrogating my son without parental consent?"

"Worth, you get back to work," he barked. "I'll be seeing you."

Then Grist laid KC's drawing on a table by the door and smiled wide like he couldn't have been happier to see Mary Green. He put both arms out like he wanted a hug, but she held out her hand for him to shake, instead.

Kneeling beside KC, Knox said, "It's none of my business, kemosabe, but I think he's moving in on your mom."

KC turned sharply on Knox, but the adults were too busy to notice. Mary glowered at Grist while Will backed his way out of the room.

"I was just talking to KC about what happened," Grist suggested innocently, as if they'd been discussing his report card instead of threatening KC with prison. "This isn't the first time he's had... a problem."

Mary's phone rang, and she snatched it open, "Ron! No, he's fine. He's all-right. Do you want to talk to him?" She frowned and shook her head at KC who'd sat up eagerly in his seat. "Yeah, he'll understand. That's what he does."

She hung up, and Grist put his hand on her shoulder. "How's the divorce coming?"

"Jeez, Charlie! We're not even separated," she shook him off to stand beside KC.

"Still just living apart? Barb and I tried that. Hey, if you ever want to talk about it..."

"Here he goes," Knox warned, and KC watched open-mouthed as Grist skulked closer.

His mom and Charlie Grist were now literally talking over KC's head, and he was helpless to do anything apart from huffing loudly and shaking his whole face in distress.

"With Bobby, my son who's in KC's class by the way, it was hard for a time. But we've been doing really well. If there's anything I can do for KC, or for you..."

"That's really very nice of you, Charlie," Mary Green tried to let Grist down easily. "I appreciate that, but--" and Grist pounced, cutting her off, "Great! Dinner Thursday? My treat."

Shaking her head, Mary stammered, "Oh, Wow, Charlie! I'm sure it would--"

"You and KC could go home now to talk, and I'd pick you up...?"

Mary glanced down at KC and grinned at him, despite his shaking his head so hard at her it looked like an earthquake was happening in between his ears.

"Okay, Charlie," she sighed. "Fine."

"Fantastic!" Grist shouted as he tousled KC's hair which KC couldn't stand.

Then he leapt over to the door, opening it up for the two of them.

He talked all the while so she couldn't take it back. "You two go on home so you can think about what you've done, son. You're suspended for the rest of the day, by the way."

"I didn't do anything," KC protested, but his mother tugged him out of the chair, eager to get him out of there.

"And I'll pick you up Thursday. 7:30?"

With Grist distracted by his mom, KC grabbed the drawing of the suspect off the desk, knowing it would be safer with him.

"Sure," she agreed again.

"But I didn't do anything!" KC still insisted.

Mary love-shoved him out the door past Grist who was smiling ear to ear, and she whispered, "C'mon, bud. Live to fight another day. Let's go."

The kids from KC's grade were returning to their classroom, and Bobby G ran up beside his father. Grist draped an arm over Bobby's shoulder, and both of them waved at the Greens with all the sincerity of politicians posing for a campaign ad.

KC kept walking with his mom, Knox beside him, but he looked back from the end of the hall to see Grist whispering to his son. Bobby cracked his knuckles and nodded as he leered at KC menacingly.

Mary Green pushed the door open without needing the push bar since the lock looked propped open, and he followed his mom outside.

Knox lingered by the exit. "I'm not an I told you so kind of fella," he I-told-you-so'd KC, "but aren't you sore you didn't tail the stranger when you had the chance?"

"No," KC shook his head, not giving the detective the satisfaction, even if he didn't believe it.

Knox flickered away with his know-it-all grin disappearing last.

"I know, bud," Mary looked back at KC sympathetically.

She must have thought he was upset about being suspended. "Charlie Grist, Mom?" KC played it off as if he was dismayed about her date, which once he got thinking about it, he absolutely was. "He's a dingus."

"Oh... KC, I was trying to help you back there."

"By going out with Charlie Grist!?"

She tsk-tsked him, "I'm not going out with him. And your father and I, you know we love each other."

"I know, and Dad knows. But do you think *Charlie* knows? Or cares?"

"Charlie's just... a friend."

KC laughed out loud.

"Okay, not a friend really--" she admitted.

"Mom, he's a dingus."

Mary tried to look stern but just wound up chuckling instead, "What is a dingus anyway?"

"I don't totally know, but it sounds right, doesn't it?"

"Maybe so, but KC your Dad and I--" he finished her sentence for her, "'Are reconciling the different things you each want?'"

He'd heard it so many times he knew the words by heart.

"Right," Mary nodded. "We want things to work out, but your dad's doing what makes him happy; and I deserve to be happy, too. Right?"

"So you think Charlie Grist will make you happy?" KC went cold.

Mary stared at her son and shook her head in disbelief, like how could this guy be so sharp most of the time and still be a little kid at heart.

"Oh, please!" she sighed. "He's a Dingus!"

KC cracked up. Then she cracked up. The two of them laughed the whole walk home because it never wasn't funny.

≈≈≈≈≈≈≈≈≈≈≈

"You stop to smell a bouquet on the way?" Knox was reclining with his back to the hall and his feet on the desk when KC came in.

KC shut the door, "What do you think's going on?"

He had been counting his footsteps til this moment when he'd get Knox alone. Ever since Grist had shown up at school to give him the third degree, he'd been imagining a conversation where he'd finally get to the bottom of what was happening.

"What I think wouldn't fill a cup of coffee," Knox responded.

After a lot of 'investigations' that mostly uncovered trouble for him and an angry phone call for his father -- from his mother -- KC and Knox were finally onto something real. *Why is Knox playing games?* KC wondered.

"Did you follow the guy?" he asked.

"It's remarkable the number of assumptions a desperate man makes when he discovers just how bad it really is," Knox answered without answering.

His non-answer drove KC crazy. "Is that a yes? Who was it?!"

Knox got up and spun his swivel chair which he must have brought with him just for the effect. "I tracked down the lead, pal, so that's for me to know and you to find out."

KC groaned and walked away while Knox needled him, "Amigo, I warned you. Needing is an addiction, and this is your cure. We've been play-acting since you were five, but if you want into the big leagues this is the price of admission. Start with what you know."

KC turned to face Knox since he wasn't a quitter. "I know there's somebody in town I've never seen before."

Knox's face seemed to tighten instead of grin as he listened, like his brain was pulling on the skin. His eyes lit up, and he nodded for KC to go on.

"I know there's a pig," KC said, and just like that the light went out on Knox's expression, even though the detective never moved a muscle.

"So what do you know?" KC interrogated Knox for a change.

"I know this is our first real case together, and real cases mean real people get hurt."

"Then why won't you be a friend?" KC practically begged.

"Call me whatever you want, kid, but a friend's just someone who hasn't crossed you yet. And right now, you and me, we're just pieces on a chess board."

KC's knees buckled, and he crumpled onto his mattress, going from frustrated to frightened in the time it took to sit down. "And pieces on a chess board, have a habit of getting knocked off," KC swallowed.

Knox nodded. The other pieces, the people of Cornelia who didn't even know they were playing a game, made KC feel too small to be responsible for a whole town. *This isn't pretend anymore.*

He remembered back to the first time he'd ever met, *really met*, Knox Chase. He was only five, but being a detective then seemed inevitable, like it would happen with or without him.

All that day, his dad had been due back from the bank any minute to help him unpack. They had to 'discuss something,' but he didn't return until late that night.

Young KC hadn't gotten much further than pulling out all of his <u>Knox Chase on the Case</u> books from the boxes. There was balled up newspaper everywhere to prove it. Then he dug out his brushes and stencils and measured out his name on the window in reverse to paint it.

Thinking back, that was a pretty absurd thing for a five-year old to do, let alone to do so well. He was determined, though, to make it perfect. To prove to his parents that everything would be okay.

He applied the last stroke just before his father got home after dark. The front door opened downstairs, and KC dropped his paint brush on the floor and hopped into bed, squealing like mad with absolutely no idea of what was about to happen to them all.

Chapter 6

ALMOST SEVEN YEARS AGO... ON THE BEST WORST NIGHT OF KC'S LIFE...

Five year old KC Green lay in bed smiling. His eyes squeezed so hard together he could see little bands of red where the bottom lids met the top ones, and he giggled. His mattress jiggled. His Dad sat down on top of the sheets that still smelled like cardboard, and the rusty springs groaned as Ron Green sighed.

KC knew that things had been rough for his folks lately. That was why they'd moved to Cornelia, a little town in the middle of nowhere where stuff was supposed to be better. None of that mattered now, though.

His dad was finally back in their house and in KC's room, and KC could hear the pages scrape open like sand paper in Ron's hands. KC sneaked a peek. It was the detective novel they'd been reading, <u>Knox Chase on the Case of the Father of the Bride</u>. Good, that was the right one. They'd stopped reading it in their old old apartment in Queens, two nights before.

His Dad's tie hung loose around his neck, and there was a bulge over his heart from the holster he must still be wearing. Being in the FBI was probably the most important job there was.

KC closed his eyes again, and his Dad cleared his throat before picking up reading where they'd left off before:

> "Saturday night traffic slicked past the detective's dark blue Oldsmobile convertible. He sat watch behind the wheel, stationed in the Bowery down the block from the dame's tenement. People called her Dorothy, but he figured none of them knew her real name either."

KC could have drawn a picture of this scene in his head without missing a single rain drop. He knew all the books by heart, but listening to his Dad read the words reassured him more than any hug ever had.

> "The occasional yellow cab fled past with its rear-windows fogged from too many couples sheltering from the storm. Sailors turning up in port with tomorrow's ex girl-friends, but tonight the ladies laughed on drenched laps like flopping fish in a net.

Knox Chase tensed behind the wind-
screen of his rag-top, waiting. A
steady drip of Winter percolated
through every seam of his canvas
roof. From each buttoned-up gap in
the fabric and everywhere the
sodden cotton sagged, icy water
trickled. It welled up in the
leather creek of his seat bench and
pooled in a lake just below his
ankles.

All that warmed him was a thermos
of something he guessed his mother
would have disapproved of, but it
kept his insides burning. That and
what he'd learned about his client,
'the Hero of Thereisenstadt.'

A diploma in a frame and a picture
in the paper are too thin to take
the measure of a man, he thought
bitterly. Knox Chase, the gumshoe,
wasn't paid for his opinions,
though.

He'd legged cases for worse clients
and smaller fees, but there was
something about this Park Avenue
phony with his white gloved
cynicism that reminded Knox of a
Cracker Jack compass he rescued

from a box once. Shiny with thick
plastic and a gilded dial,
evidently no matter where you
pointed the thing you were facing
due north.

He'd locked it in the drawer of his
desk with other tools of the trade,
because it reminded him that every
Joe is telling the truth... If
you're dumb enough to believe him.

Then the third floor window he'd
been watching clicked faintly to
life, and a frown creased his lips.
Knox Chase stepped into the down-
pour, wondering why this dame had
gone in the back door but
nevertheless turned on the light."

KC Green opened his eyes, expecting his dad to keep
reading. He couldn't stop now, KC thought, *my heart's
killing me.*

Knox Chase on the Case had been his dad's hero
since back when he was KC's age. He always said so,
but tonight the words tripped over his father's tongue
without the usual rat-a-tat discharge he had when his
heart was in it.

Ron hunched on the edge of KC's old-fashioned bed
while his son puppy-eye pleaded for him to read a few

pages more. He wouldn't whine, not KC, but he did resemble man's-best-friend resting his chin on your lap beneath the dinner table.

"What happens next, Dad?"

Ron smiled, despite himself, and he glanced down at the book in his lap like he was going to start reading again. KC flung himself back onto his pillow, eyes snapping closed with a big grin, expecting the detective story.

Behind his eyelids, he could picture the rain-soaked private eye glaring at him hard from inside the pages. He was flickery and black-and-white and loomed over you like he was up on an old-fashioned movie screen. Knox Chase was gritty like a mountain painted on a brick wall, and wrapped in his trench coat and fedora you could never tell what discoveries were buttoned behind his lips.

Knox's jaw clenched just then, but the detective winked at him. *That's funny.* His pulp fiction name-sake had never done *that* before, *but maybe it was just the rain?* That's what KC figured.

Instead of going on, Ron Green cleared a big lump in his throat in a way that told his son he was in store for something other than a story. "KC, we have to talk."

Behind KC's eye-lids, Knox muttered, "I'm waiting..."

"I wanted the whole day with you, Pal, but something happened at the bank, and I had to take care of it. I'm sorry," Ron began, and KC opened his eyes and cut him off. "What happened? Did somebody try to stick it up?"

Ron frowned, "Not exactly a stick-up, but there was an attempted robbery."

"And you caught them?!"

"I was in the right place to catch 'em. Yup. But that kept me from being in the right place to help you get your room squared away and all these boxes unpacked..."

"Who cares, Dad!? You stopped an actual hold-up!" KC leapt up in bed and squeezed his father as hard as he could, burying his face in the valley of his dad's jacket between the tips of his shoulder blades. "Who cares about the boxes? We'll empty them after school tomorrow! I promise..."

KC kept hugging his dad. His dad had actually *apprehended* a bank robber. On his first day in Cornelia, he was already a hero! That's why *his* dad was who KC wanted to be when he grew up.

Ron Green squeezed his son's hand and looked over his shoulder to meet his gaze, "You're going to have to empty the boxes without me, KC. I leave tomorrow."

KC nodded to let his Dad know it was okay, "I'll put all my stuff up, Daddy. Don't worry."

"Thanks, Pal," Ron Green sniffled, his eyes getting shiny.

KC studied his Dad's face as Ron Green wiped at his nose with the back of his hand. "When will you be back?"

"You know that at the Bureau, where I work, everybody has important jobs to do?"

KC blinked, and when he blinked, he could see Knox Chase still standing in the rain, grumbling, "Waiting right here where you left me..."

"At the Bureau, even though every job is important, maybe the most important is the guy who goes undercover to catch the bad guys. Do you know what undercover means?" Ron asked.

KC thought it meant that his father would be gone for a long time. He nodded.

"It means that I have to pretend to *be* a bad guy, but don't worry, KC, I won't *do* anything bad. I just have to pretend. It's okay to pretend if you're doing it to help people."

KC's face was burning. He was breathing so fast it was incredible any air was getting to his head. His fingers were tingling, and he felt dizzy, but he wouldn't let himself fall down on the bed, so he steadied himself on his father's shoulder.

"KC, are you okay?"

"Do you know when you'll be back, Dad?"

Ron Green started to answer with a big reassuring smile, and it looked like he was about to say something like 'Don't worry!' or 'You won't even notice I'm gone,' or 'It'll be okay...,' but KC was looking at him so hard he must have decided not to pretend. Not to him.

"No," Ron said. "It *could* be a few months. Or it could be... longer."

KC smiled. He felt like his cheeks were going to collapse from propping them up so hard, and he was shaking all over in his pajamas so much he suddenly had to go to the bathroom, urgently, but he knew his Dad's job needed him.

His mom definitely needed him, too, because KC knew she got really sad sometimes, but he wasn't going to let his father down by complaining. KC inhaled in a deep breath and blinked hard to keep himself from peeing.

With his eyes closed, he saw the black and white city block in the Bowery. He saw the rain and the old car and the run-down buildings, *but there was no Knox Chase.*

KC blinked open and looked hard in Ron Green's eyes to promise, "I'll take care of Mommy, Dad. Don't worry!"

Ron Green's face caved in, and he breathed in deep with tears running down his cheeks and a little snot bubbling up in his nose. He hugged KC so tightly his son couldn't breathe.

Over Ron's shoulder, Knox Chase flashed into KC's room and then disappeared. Then he reappeared. Off and on, again and again, like a fluorescent tube coming to life until he just looked... there. Still flickering like an old movie image in black and white but like he wasn't going anywhere.

Knox Chase nodded at KC like this was the place he was meant to be. He tipped his wet hat with rain water that never quite hit the floor, and KC smiled at the detective guiltily as he hugged his father back.

"I love you, KC," Ron Green told him.

"Copy that," KC answered, not yet ready to let go. He wanted to hold onto his Dad as long as he could.

Chapter 7

If he'd known then what he knew now, maybe KC wouldn't have gone into the private eye game. People getting hurt was way more than he'd signed up for.

He closed his eyes and fell back on top of his unmade sheets, groaning "What do you want from me?"

Knox didn't say anything for a minute. The detective turned to stare out the window.

"Would it be enough for us to do some good?" he eventually answered like it was really a question.

If KC had been looking, he'd have seen a glimmer of fear in his hero's eyes. That was something that had never been there before in their almost seven year whatever-it-was. Lids shut tight, though, KC didn't notice and kept thinking of how his Dad still hadn't solved *his* case after three years and thousands of miles trying.

It had taken Ron Green two years just to figure out he was looking for one criminal genius instead of dozens of patsies. This mastermind had pinned the blame on a different fall-guy in every city and town where there'd been a heist while getting away with tens of millions in stolen jewels. Meanwhile, the people doing time for his crimes didn't even know who'd framed them.

Lately this thief had begun taunting KC's Dad who only had a set of initials and a trail of broken lives to go on. Worst of all, Ron Green knew he was running out of time before the FBI took the case away from him.

KC wondered what if it took *him* years to figure out what was happening in Cornelia and lots of people got hurt while he was trying? The spit in his mouth suddenly tasted metallic because his stomach was churning overtime. He lay there worrying *if none of these 'grown-ups' is grown-up enough to solve a real problem, what am I supposed to do? How do I save this town from a person -- I DON'T KNOW WHO -- doing something -- I DON'T KNOW WHAT -- some time -- I DON'T EVEN KNOW WHEN?!*

KC decided *I CAN NOT, N-O-T, DO THIS,* and in that exact instant Knox Chase was swept off his feet and tugged backwards, almost sucked into himself. Like he was being vacuumed into an old fashioned TV tube that was powering down because someone had flipped a switch.

He tried to shout for KC, but it came out as a tiny squeak before fading off entirely. Meanwhile, Knox was squeezed, spun and shrunken into a tiny white dot that popped brilliantly and then dissolved away until nothing was left but the red memory you get from looking at something too bright.

KC opened his eyes to plead for a hint or something, but it was too late. He was all alone. Knox was gone.

≈≈≈≈≈≈≈≈≈≈≈

> Staring up at Dorothy's fourth
> floor window, a million stories
> flickered on the screen in Knox
> Chase's head, and none of them had
> a happy ending for the dame. I'm
> not getting any drier out here in
> the rain, he thought to himself as
> he dodged Niagara Falls to huddle
> outside the vestibule door.

Knox Chase was back on the Case of the Father of the Bride without any idea why. Stuck playing a part like a harlequin on strings, he was performing the motions, phoning them in. How he got there and how he could get back to KC were just two of the mysteries pinballing through his head.

> Glancing in both directions before
> picking up a small piece of slate
> from the crumbling side-walk, Knox
> tried the door handle and surveyed
> the lock. He figured he could have
> picked the thing clean in a couple
> of minutes. I've got all the time
> in the world, but what about her?

That was all the reasoning it took before he bashed in the door's glass window to twist the knob from within. Ordinarily he'd have discarded the rock, but something told him it would be welcome in his pocket along with the gun he didn't bring.

Inside, he discovered no expense had ever been spent to improve the building or the lives of its residents. The place was filthy and falling down brick by cinder. The elevator shaft was missing doors... and an elevator, but the stairs built around it still seemed to be in working order. Knox took them two at a time, careful to keep the scuff of his step to a minimum. He made it up to the girl's floor in short order.

Her room was the one at the end of the hall on the street side. He'd been watching from his car for so long a map of his seat cushions was monogrammed beneath his wet slacks. None of that told him what he'd find in her apartment, though.

Tailing this dame for so long and admiring the curve in her hip and the snicker of her lips, he'd imagined meeting 'Dorothy' under more auspicious circumstances. For both of them.

He put his ear to the thick walnut door, covered in so many shades of the same cheap blue paint that the stuff never dried so much as solidified into viscous jelly. He could read enough dull fingerprints pressed into the surface that if he'd still been on the force he could have cleared a year's backlog just from evidence of her comings and goings. Through the thick wood, though, all he heard was a muffled female voice and the sound of a footstep before the door knob in Knox's hand twisted open from the inside.

Chapter 8

*AFTER VALENTINE'S DAY... THE INVESTIGATION
BEGINS...*

KC was distracted enough the next day that he didn't
really notice Knox was nowhere to be found. The
hurting, however, that his friend, *or maybe we're not even
friends*, had promised seemed to have gotten a jump-start
while KC was home sulking.

He opened his classroom door and spotted Cat
behind her desk in a wrist cast that ended just below her
left elbow. It made KC ache as soon as he saw it. The
heels of her shoes burrowed against the edge of her
chair, and she wrapped up her legs in both arms, the
good one and the bad one, and she avoided his gaze
when he tried to make eye contact.

He wanted to go over and ask her about it, and ask
her if she was okay and ask her if there was anything he
could do and tell her that... but of course he didn't even
know if he'd be able to get a word out. He never could
around her, so he just looked at her, hurting.

The bell rang, and he was still staring at her. Mrs.
Pepper had to walk over and put a hand on his shoulder

and whisper quietly for to him to take his seat. Everyone seemed subdued that morning. Bobby G was atypically quiet with his chubby lips pursed and his normally-snickering companions silent.

KC made his way into the second row of polygon shaped tables and sat down next to Benjy, who looked away.

"Class, as most of you seem to already know, Mr. Ringmeyer has been in an accident," Mrs. Pepper began gently.

KC barely registered the news about the chorus teacher, because he couldn't figure out what was happening with his friend, "Are you not talking to me now?" KC whispered, and Benjy just frowned back at him.

"Et tu, Benjy?" KC persisted as Mrs. Pepper went on in the background. Their class had done Julius Caesar for the Fall play.

"Right before this big concert, we're extraordinarily lucky to have a highly qualified replacement...," the teacher said.

Benjy relented, but he had to look down at his feet to speak with KC, "My mom says that you're having a tough time and that I should give you time to work your issues out on your own."

"How does your Mom even know about my 'tough time?'" KC asked, already knowing the answer.

For someone who seemed so slick and self-sufficient, Benjy was this new-age kid who told his parents *everything*. He lived in a family where feelings were like food and everyone was always hungry.

"How come she doesn't want you to help me work through my 'tough time' feelings?" KC asked sarcastically. "Don't my feelings matter to her? And to you?"

He looked at himself in the trench coat he'd bought two sizes too big on his 10th birthday and in the hat his dad mailed with a card on his 11th birthday, and he suddenly felt like a giant odd-ball. It was no use getting mad at Benjy's mom. She was a nice lady, and who could blame her for not wanting her son to hang-out with a trouble-making turd? *Why do I even do it?* he asked himself, *make myself into a laughing-stock for a fiction that's maybe just in my head...?*

Then he glanced back across the room at Cat sitting there with her hand in a cast, and the sight of her hurting yanked him out of his self-pity. He turned with new determination back to Benjy.

"Okay, forget about me," he whispered more insistently, "What happened to Cat?"

Benjy squirmed in his seat. To KC it looked like there was even more story here than he expected.

"Because the concert is so important, you will have extra chorus today..." Mrs. Pepper went on.

"I feel a little guilty about it," Benjy began, "but it was kind of your fault."

KC felt like he'd been poked in both eyes. He had to swallow back a shout. The idea that he'd somehow hurt Cat was enough to make him die on the inside.

Meanwhile, Mrs. Pepper informed them there would be a field trip the next day, but KC couldn't hear her because he was waiting for his friend to go on. Benjy saw the ache in his face and told him the whole story.

At recess yesterday, after KC had gotten thrown out of school, Benjy said that Bobby G and his gang had taken it upon themselves to 'interrogate' him. Twisting his arm behind his back, the 'interrogation' consisted of trying to make Benjy say that KC was crazy. They were really just torturing him for no good reason.

"Say it!" Bobby G shouted.

"It was just-- a card," Benjy gasped, his face practically in the grass and them twisting his hand even further behind him. "And he's not the one breaking my arm."

Benjy said he'd screamed loud enough to break a window it hurt so much, and then out of nowhere Cat showed up and shoved Bobby G out of the way.

Bobby G asked her, "What did you do that for?" and she said, "Demonstrating cause and effect."

Then she pushed him down, knocking him to the ground. "I hit you, and you hit the dirt, jerk."

She pulled Benjy back to his feet. "But that's when Bobby G snuck up on her and pushed her from behind," Benjy said, making KC's mouth open in horror. "She tripped on a rock and tried to stop herself, and her wrist snapped."

"He pushed a girl? With her back turned?" KC asked, dumbfounded. "Typical Grist."

Benjy nodded.

Mrs. Pepper told everyone to get up, that they were heading for emergency choir practice. KC was too paralyzed with hatred to do what she said. There was nothing he wanted more than a chance to get even, and as chairs scraped all around with kids rushing to the door, Bobby G was suddenly looming over him.

"I'm watching you, Psycho," Bobby G swore.

KC rocketed out of his seat and looked right back in Bobby's eyes, breathing like he was on the 11th kilometer of a 10k race, and he said, "Bobby, in kindergarten when you were still eating paste, you sounded so much smarter with your mouth glued shut."

Everybody laughed. Everybody was watching them.

Bobby hauled back to punch KC, but Mrs. Pepper grabbed his arm and said, "Is there a problem, Bobby?!"

The whole time, KC didn't flinch. Bobby could have been three times bigger instead of just two times bigger, and KC wouldn't have backed down.

Bobby shook his head to the teacher and marched with the other kids at the head of the line to the music room. Meanwhile, Cat watched as KC and Benjy went to the back of the line, heading out the door and snaking down the hall. A hard look burned in her eyes.

KC told Benjy "I'm not asking you to disobey your mother, and if you think I'm crazy, so be it."

Benjy looked at him and said, "I don't think you're crazy, exactly. Maybe you're just working through feelings of loss and abandonment? That could explain your delusions."

Oh Jeez! KC all-of-a-sudden realized things with Benjy were worse than he'd guessed. He looked around for Knox so he could see the trouble their investigations were causing for him, but Knox Chase was still nowhere to be seen.

"Just like that," Benjy whispered. "You're looking for someone right now, aren't you?"

"There's nobody here," KC chuckled. "What are you talking about?"

Benjy seemed ready to tell KC that he *knew* what he was talking about, but they were interrupted before he could. Cat had hung back in order to join them.

"Hi," she said, looking like she had something to get off her chest.

Lorrie and Cat's other friends, up ahead in line, whispered intensely the second Cat joined them. It sounded like a million mice nibbling a million pieces of cheese.

"What are you guys talking about?" Cat went on, sounding indifferent to what people must have been gossiping.

Benjy was about to tell her, but KC shook his head at him so sharply he just said, "Oh, hi..."

Then KC swallowed hard and nodded at Cat, but he couldn't make eye contact. She was too amazing to be eye to eye with this close, so he looked away, listening in fear to his stomach gurgling from all the awkwardness, convinced she could hear it.

Just then, more than anything, KC wanted some advice. *Where IS Knox when I need him?* He looked around but couldn't find any sign of the detective who hardly ever left his side.

"You don't talk?" Cat demanded in KC's face.

She planted her feet in front of his and crossed her arms, daring him to knock her over. So KC stopped, and Benjy stopped too, a smile forming at the corners of his mouth.

"I... It's just--" KC stammered back, still afraid to look her in the eyes.

"Or you just won't talk to a girl...?" She demanded, "And what did you mean 'give me the piggy,' anyway?"

She really believed I wrote that stupid note to her. That did it.

KC looked up and met her stare for stare, square in the eyes. "I have no idea. I didn't write that! I would never write something like that to you. Or to anyone."

Cat was about to challenge him, but he talked right over her, "Somebody is doing something terrible, and we're going to find out who it is," he gestured to Benjy who was watching open-mouthed as his friend was suddenly talking to the girl of his dreams. "And we're gonna stop 'em, right?"

"Right," Benjy answered before he could even think better of it.

Suddenly, Knox Chase flickered into being from nothing. Stuttering into sight slowly at first, he built up speed until he was a dripping wet, heavy-breathing delusion in the sort-of-flesh. He shook his head like there was something stuck between his ears, and he looked around trying to figure out what he was doing in KC's school's hallway, but he was back.

KC glanced at him, too wrapped up in this new mission to notice much about the state Knox was in, and he muttered "About time" as he walked past Cat to rejoin the kids up ahead.

Benjy went with him, smiling in astonishment. Knox stayed behind and watched as Cat shook her head and laughed, impressed by the kid she'd just finally met after five years of knowing him.

Then he caught up to KC to ask "How'd we get here? And when did you start breaking hearts, chum?"

KC didn't know what Knox was talking about, and before he could figure it out Benjy started pounding him with celebratory punches. "Way to go, man. Wow!" Benjy shouted as Cat caught up to them at a run.

"Okay," she demanded. "What's your plan?"

She was right beside KC, and he glanced past her to the still dripping Knox Chase who didn't seem so okay.

"Don't look at me," the detective shrugged, a far-away stare in his eyes as water droplets fell from his hat only to disappear in mid-air. "Last thing I knew you were asking what I wanted from you, and then...," and he shook his head, unable to go on.

"We're working on it," KC insisted. He had no idea what Knox was talking about.

"All-right," Cat seemed to consider for a split second. "Then I'm in *IF* you help me figure out a plan of my own."

"To do what?" Benjy asked.

They arrived at the door to the chorus room and looked inside where Bobby G and his buddies were kicking some smaller kids out of their chairs in the front row.

She rubbed her cast and nodded in their direction. "To get even."

Benjy couldn't help himself but smile. KC and Cat looked into one another's eyes and shook on it. Then all three of them walked into class together, leaving Knox behind to pat himself down, frowning, as he checked to see if he was all there.

Chapter 9

The chorus room was ringed by built-in bleachers, four tiers high. They surrounded the piano and the stage, and kids were climbing the risers to take their seats.

Mrs. Pepper stood in the middle of the room, smiling with too many teeth showing from being nice to a sour-faced woman none of them had seen before. This visitor scowled and huffed, open-mouthed, while her foot jack-hammered the floor like there were a million more important places she had to be.

Fed up, their teacher turned away and spotted someone walking in behind KC, Cat and Benjy. She waved, gratefully, in her direction, and the kids turned and glimpsed a beautiful young lady who happened to be passing through Knox Chase at that very instant.

Mrs. Pepper sighed with relief, "Here she is! Our savior... This is Miss Sosaurus -- rhymes with thesaurus?"

This pretty woman lit up with the most gracious smile ever as she nodded YES. Only a few inches taller than Benjy, one of the taller kids in their grade, she could have passed for a member of their class even if she was probably in her early 20s. She bubbled with medium chestnut hair that was probably blond in the summer.

Benjy gushed to KC as she walked by, "That's our sub?! She's beautiful..." which made her blush.

Ms. Sosaurus shook Mrs. Pepper's hand, and she effused to the whole class, "You're soooo sweet, but you guys can just call me Bridget, okay?"

Then Bridget Sosaurus turned back to Mrs. Pepper and saw the frown and tiny shake of the older teacher's head, and she revised, "Or maybe just call me Miss Bridget? Or Miss Sosaurus?" Her innocent titters were infectious. "Just don't call me late for dinner, all-right?"

Mrs. Pepper beamed. All the kids laughed, and more than a few of the boys grinned and looked away from her rosy-cheeked smile. She was so pretty.

Everyone lit up except the sharply dressed lady Mrs. Pepper had been speaking with. This woman's dark skin and black hair made her look like she was from India, and though really fit and skinny and healthy-looking in general, just then she seemed sick enough to be in intensive care.

She held a wad of crumpled tissues under her runny red nose, and her wet eyes bulged with drippy sickness. The deep, dark bags beneath them made her look like a St. Bernard. If she'd been smiling and healthy you would have described her as pretty, but right then, her grimace was more zombie than cover girl.

"Miss Sosaurus, this is Oona Peshey," Mrs. Pepper introduced her, but the sick lady interrupted, "P-E-S-C-E. It's pronounced pesh like mesh."

"Sorry- She's here with the museum, to make sure... of something, I'm-I'm not sure--"

Ms. Pesce sighed, "I'm here to either cancel this concert on Saturday or--"

"You can't cancel the concert!" Ms. Sosaurus cut her off, "What about these kids?!"

The kids had been looking forward to this concert for months, and Mr. Ringmeyer gave them the assignment of listening to his Mikado mash-up over Christmas, so most of them already knew the words. Though they'd only had one rehearsal so far, Cat had sung like an angel and could already perform the show on the piano without needing sheet music. Not that she could play the piano on Saturday anymore.

"Ultimately, that's a decision the Cornelia Art Museum will have to make," Ms. Pesce conceded. "I represent the lending institution, and it's my responsibility to make sure that no matter how small the exhibitor, that it live up to every obligation in the loan agreement, and this--."

"What does that mean, exactly?" Bridget interrupted, her eyebrows scrunching together.

"It means that this sort of thing," Ms. Pesce waved her snot-covered tissue at the kids, and more broadly at their town and the ridiculous concert they'd been planning to perform, "seems marginal. At best. With their chorus teacher out of the picture, I don't see how the children of Roosevelt Elementary can participate in the Opening Ceremony."

The kids all murmured to one another with heads drooping, and Mrs. Pepper flushed, but it was Ms. Sosaurus who stepped forward in a rush.

"They'll be ready," she swore. "I'll make sure of it."

It was inspiring to see how seriously she was taking this thing.

"We'll see," was all that Oona Pesce managed before a sneezing fit overcame her, and she staggered out the door and down the hall without squeezing in a goodbye, just waving behind her as she went.

"We'll be ready!" Ms. Sosaurus enthused. "Won't we, kids! We'll show her!"

"Absolutely we will!" Benjy shouted back.

It made most kids giggle, but everyone shared the sentiment, and Bridget Sosaurus smiled so warmly at Benjy that if he'd been made of butter someone would have had to mop the floor to wipe him up. KC tugged his jiggly arm three times just to get him to look away from their substitute and head for their seats in the middle of the second row. Cat joined them since she wouldn't be accompanying the class on the piano.

When they got to their chairs, Benjy couldn't quite bring himself to sit down. He just kind of hovered half-way over his seat, getting redder by the second, gaping at Miss Sosaurus until he folded himself down sideways, never taking his eyes off of her.

"Is he always like this?" Cat asked KC.

KC shrugged. He was caught off-guard by Ms. Sosaurus, too, but he buzzed even more from just sitting next to Cat. Heck, he was talking to her. This was already thirty times more words than he'd managed to say to her over the previous five years combined.

Mrs. Pepper smiled at Miss Sosaurus, "You've got just four days to get them ready, so you've got your work cut out for you. Kids, do whatever Miss Sosaurus says. Understood?"

"We're gonna have so much fun," Bridget put her hand on Mrs. Pepper's shoulder to reassure her, and KC could hear Benjy sigh beside him.

"That's the spirit," Mrs. Pepper smiled before heading out the door, passing through Knox, who was still discombobulated. She called behind her, "If you'll bring these song-birds back to home-room before lunch? See you, guys."

"Bye, Mrs. Pepper."

KC watched Knox still checking himself out, feeling around in his pockets and rolling his shoulders as if trying to work out a sore muscle, and he *was* dripping wet.

KC shot his partner an inquiring look, and Knox answered queasily "I don't know."

Then Bridget bounded towards the doorway, floating on the balls of her feet like a ballerina on stage. She eased the door closed quietly, and just like that, Knox was gone.

She spun conspiratorially and smiled to the kids in the class like she was letting them in on a secret. "This is a very important concert. Right?"

She stage whispered so all the kids leaned forward to hear. Almost everyone nodded.

Cat didn't. Maybe she was with-holding judgment on the substitute, or it could have been something in Miss Sosaurus' tone that seemed too touchy-feely. Whatever it was, it was enough for KC to hang back as well, since he could tell Cat was skeptical.

"On stage and in life, it's important to show people what you can do. What you're made of." She looked in every face she could reach as if she were delivering the mystery of existence with this speech. Then she asked in a voice no louder than a breath, "What do you think?"

The thing was, she was inspiring and mysterious and so pretty that most of the kids nodded, and some were too spell-bound to answer.

Benjy, however, was so overwhelmed with emotion he declared, "Uh-Hunh-RIGHT!" and it came out of his throat as a poly-syllabic croak instead of actual words.

Bridget grinned and tiptoed over to him with feline precision.

Almost purring, she leaned in, "That's so super to hear you say, sweetie, because I need a few volunteers, for-" Benjy's hand rocketed out of his lap before she could even finish her sentence.

It happened so fast, KC was still trying to figure out why Miss Bridget had stopped talking when he realized Benjy was staring at him, armpit straining with fingers shaking in mid-air. Benjy's look pleaded that a real buddy would raise his hand right now, too. So KC did, and after a groan which let everyone know she was doing so under protest, Cat joined in.

Bridget grinned. "--For making posters?! Do you wanna make big posters for the concert?"

Benjy nodded like a puppy, but making big posters was about the last thing KC wanted to do. He deadpanned, "great" at the exact same time Cat did, and the two turned and smiled at each other, "Jinx!"

"Then it's settled," Bridget went on, digging into her purse, "Get the biggest paper you can find. 10 feet long, 4 feet wide and at least 4 sheets. That'll show 'em we mean business."

"You want us to decorate one hundred-sixty square feet of poster?" Cat asked, astonished by the math and the waste of time it represented.

Bridget smiled dreamily and unfurled a $50 bill, dangling it for Benjy to take, "And keep the change..."

Everyone else in the class muttered as Benjy took the crisp money and winked at Bridget. "The name's Ben by the way," he intoned in a deeper voice than KC had ever heard from his friend.

Bridget smiled, but Cat cracked up. Even KC did a double-take, but Benjy was utterly unselfconscious about it, intent on making a really impressive first impression.

Miss Sosaurus nodded and turned to go as KC leaned over to whisper, "Thanks, Cat, for joining in. At least we can dig--,"

Miss Sosaurus spun back around and cut him off before he could say *for clues*. "Cat? Catarina Liszt? My piano player?"

It was the first time Ms. Sosaurus' smile had failed her. Staring at Cat's cast, Bridget just shook her head slowly back and forth.

"I broke it yesterday," Cat nodded.

Bobby G sniggered to his friends in front of her.

"I'm really sorry, kiddo," Bridget frowned sympathetically before mustering a *show must go on* smile and looking around the room and belting out, "So who's gonna play for me?"

Not a single hand went up. None of the kids was willing to touch Cat's piano. Even the folks who'd been taking lessons since the womb knew they couldn't tickle the ivories like she did. The keys might as well have read *Property of Catarina A. Liszt -- Don't Bother!*

"Play the scales...? Or something?" Bridget's smile was collapsing as all the would-be piano players slunk down in their chairs to get out of the job. "Well, that's fine," she bucked up with show-biz bravado, "Because today we'll focus on warming up. Properly."

Cat raised an eyebrow and muttered, "for three hours?"

KC shrugged, having no idea how long you were supposed to warm up.

"Let's hear it. Don't be bashful," Bridget beamed at them. "Your usual warm-ups... Now.... Go... Start."

Bridget implored them with her gaze, but no one's diaphragm budged, so she went to the piano and tapped a few keys discordantly and waved her hand in the air dramatically.

"La-la-la-la-la-la-LA!" The kids started singing.

It was very off-key.

Bridget just smiled, "That's the spirit! Again."

The kids ascended the scale even more off-key, but instead of wincing Bridget smiled wider, "Wonderful. Even higher!"

From the hall, Will Worth looked through the tiny window built into the door as they tried to break the glass with their screechy scales. A frown crossed his expression as he saw KC. Their eyes met, and Will broke away guiltily. He lumbered off, dragging his mop and bucket with Knox Chase close behind.

Chapter 10

It really was a 3-hour warm up. It was like they were rehearsing their rehearsal, and as much fun as it usually is to get a break from classes, by the end of the morning everyone was ready to get the heck out of the chorus room. Everyone except Benjy.

He could have warmed up with Ms. Sosaurus all day, everyday. The rest of school he kept grinning in moon-faced, drift away daydreams, no doubt about their substitute teacher. KC even tried to tease him about it, but Benjy was unrepentant.

"Yeah, I really like her," he nodded.

It was no fun picking on someone who agreed with you whole-heartedly, but KC tried needling him again, "Now who's imagining things."

Benjy just beamed back at him, "Yeah..."

Walking into town after school to begin their investigation, though, Cat was livid, "Can you believe that chorus class?"

"What?!" Benjy stammered, genuinely surprised. "It was good. I liked her."

"Obviously...," KC chuckled, thinking back to when Benjy had kidded him for liking Cat.

She changed tactics, delicately, "But do you think... she knows anything about music? I mean--"

Benjy jumped down her throat, "She's filling in for Mr. Ringmeyer who picked a lousy time to take a break."

"He broke his leg... Getting hit by a car, and she couldn't even play the piano... I mean..." Cat lectured just short of yelling.

"Mr. Ringmeyer got hit by a car?" KC interrupted her.

They were in front of Mr. Jenkins' store and KC wasn't too eager to go see him anymore, plus he hadn't realized *that* was what had happened to their teacher. He and Benjy stopped next to the metal trash cans by the curb as Knox Chase flickered into being, suddenly interested too.

"Now we're getting somewhere," he said.

"Weren't you listening this morning?" Cat asked, pulling the door open enough to make the little shop bell tinkle.

"Wait!" KC tried stopping her. "Mr. Jenkins could be busy or..."

"Recuperating?" Benjy suggested. "KC knocked him out of a tree two days ago."

"You did? Mr. Jenkins??" Cat was horrified.

"His branch broke," KC demanded.

"Yeah, after you pelted him with wood chips," Benjy agreed, making Knox snicker.

"I thought he was looking in people's windows, and I was trying to stop him," KC growled for Knox's benefit. "And anyway, do you actually think the guy with the note's gonna be here?"

"Hang on. Do you think the suspect came out of this building or not?" Cat insisted.

Knox laughed, "She's got pep!"

"You said it," KC muttered under his breath, suddenly aware of the conversation he was apparently having with himself. "Uh, yeah. Yes, I mean."

Cat wrinkled her brows at KC and then turned to walk through the door, "Then, we've got to ask Mr. Jenkins some questions."

Benjy followed, shaking his head, "You really need some help, man."

When the other two were inside, KC muttered, "Thanks for making me look like a lunatic in front of Cat."

"At least somebody wants to get to the bottom of this," Knox snapped.

"Wait here," KC grumbled as he went inside, and Knox called after him, "Then pay attention for both of us because I'm not getting any younger."

The little shop's interior was a porcelain assault on the senses. Transparent shelves lined walls overflowing with figurines and china plates. Racks and cube cases brimmed with delicate tchotchkes and chintz covered bric-a-brac from the 1800s. Wooden carved keepsakes lurked everywhere.

Commanding pride of place when shoppers tiptoed in was an ancient four-masted clipper. Its sails billowed inside a narrow necked, leaded glass jug. This ship had actually been built *within* the bottle, not just put there, and between the *Not For Sale* sign in front of it and the ornate stand it was on, this was clearly *very* expensive.

Jenkins' store was the kind of place that should have been really dusty, but despite having not enough space to turn yourself around in without bumping into something, every millimeter glistened. It was like one hundred grandmothers had built a massive curio cabinet and then linked feather dusters to keep it spotless.

A voice moaned from the back of the store, "Just a second... So sorry I'm taking so long. The other night, I had a small accident."

Benjy and Cat stared at KC. He blushed. Mr. Jenkins' groans, accompanied by metal creaks and rubber thuds, scuffled closer until two cane tips appeared on a carpet behind a large cabinet.

"Mr. Jenkins?" Cat asked.

His kindly voice disappeared. "No children," he shouted, still rounding the bend.

"No children!" he repeated louder, and then he took a good look at KC standing in his lobby, and he hissed "Especially No *You*!"

Mr. Jenkins was wearing a cervical collar and some sort of back brace which wrapped up tight around his body like a truss. KC backed away, mumbling his apologies, headed toward the door when the kitten from the night before leapt into his arms.

Mr. Jenkins screamed, "Put Petunia down!"

KC froze, "Okay, Mr. Jenkins. Of course! Yes, and we've got a couple of questions if you'll--," but the antiques dealer wasn't listening.

He turned on Benjy angrily, waving one of his canes in his face. "You must be that Knox he was talking to. His partner in terror."

Benjy forgot about Mr. Jenkins and his cane, and his head swiveled towards KC. The only thing wider than Benjy's stare was his open mouth, which struggled like the rest of his expression to find words for what he was thinking. KC went so white you might have thought he'd suffered a vampire bite. Meanwhile, Jenkins' glare darted between the two of them, and his wavering cane swooped through the air, inches from their faces.

Cat seized Petunia from KC and put the kitten back on the ground, exclaiming, "Mr. Jenkins, who are you renting the upstairs apartment to?"

He turned on her, "That's none of your business, miss."

"We need to speak with the man up there. It's urgent."

His nose wrinkled like he'd caught a whiff of something terrible as he insisted, "There's no *man* up there. Imagine! I'd never rent my apartment to some man."

"What do you mean?" Benjy turned back towards Mr. Jenkins, who stomped the ground with his cane and inched closer to the kids every time he rattled off a rule for NOT renting his apartment.

"NO children. NO families. And NO Men!" The last was the most important and got the biggest pounding, and when he finished he was towering over them and had scared Petunia so badly, the kitten scampered up onto a shelf over their heads where she trembled next to the china plates. "The havoc a single man would wreak on all my things...," Jenkins laughed humorlessly.

"You only rent to women?" Cat accused him. "That's discrimination. You can't do that."

"And you can't come into my store," Jenkins hollered in each of their faces until every vein in his cheeks popped blue. "Out! Shoo, the lot of you!"

It looked like his cervical collar was trapping all the blood in his head, and droplets of spittle clung to his quivering lip. Cat backed away from him with KC and Benjy already one step closer to the door. Mr. Jenkins wobbled precariously after her, enraged, waggling both of his canes in the air.

The cane tips bobbled inches from priceless treasures on either side of the store as he roared, red-faced, at the kids, "Out!"

With this last shout, though, Mr. Jenkins lost his balance and stumbled, his butt bumping the *Not For Sale* ship in a bottle. The jug wobbled, then teetered then toppled off its plinth, sailing to the ground on its final voyage.

Jenkins hollered "No...!" to no avail.

The protruding cork smacked the floor first, and the wooden ship within disintegrated to cinders, but the bottle was okay until the entire assemblage bounced. This time the jug landed on its side and shattered with a loud pop which scared Petunia out of her wits.

The kitten tore off down the china shelf, swishing an entire row of antique dishes with her tail as she sprinted. One by one, plate after plate tinkled in a bell-like ring as it pinged into the floor below, bursting into blue and pink dust.

Jenkins shrieked higher and higher with every dish. "Petunia, Bad Kitty!" he sobbed after her, and then he turned on the kids wailing "Bad Kiddies!"

KC, Benjy and Cat held each other in terror as the antiques dealer howled. He flailed after them with his cane as if bopping them on their noggins was all he had left to live for. The kids kept backing their way out the door, onto the side-walk, and wouldn't stop until they'd knocked over the trash-cans on the curb and had fallen into the fresh garbage they'd scattered everywhere.

Chapter 11

A Clue by Any Other Name... Would Smell Just As Stinky...

Smash. After the clatter of knocking four metal garbage cans down to the ground, denting two of them with their behinds and landing in left-over dinners and discarded magazines, Benjy groaned.

Knox hovered over KC, smirking, "That's one way to get to the bottom of this," while KC stewed, angry about how his 'friend' was making him look bad.

Cat just laughed, though, "And to think I'd be home practicing piano right now if not for Bobby G."

She was enjoying herself despite the fish bones and piles of papers that had toppled all over the sidewalk and into the street.

Benjy started cleaning everything up, and while gathering the magazines he noticed a letter had been cut out of one of the covers of <u>Antiquities Quarterly</u>. "Hey guys!" he said, "What do you make of this?"

They each got up, and Knox Chase angled closer to see what they'd uncovered. Leafing through all the pages, they found dozens of holes in a bunch of issues where someone had cut capital letters out. Possibly to construct a ransom note, or maybe even more than one.

"I think that the stranger who wrote that letter really was here," Cat said, looking at KC like if there'd been any doubt about him, she was totally convinced of his innocence now.

"And he might know Mr. Jenkins' tenant," KC tucked one of the magazines into his bag for evidence.

Benjy grinned, "Maybe Mr. Jenkins is up to some funny business? Could be he deserved to get knocked out of that tree."

"I didn't--" KC began to shout but stopped himself and took a breath "I told you, it was gravity. Not me."

Knox watched this investigation by committee quietly, making no comment. Though, KC could tell he was deep in thought.

Then Cat chimed in after mulling it over, "It's possible, but he didn't seem like he was faking those injuries, so I don't think KC bumped into him yesterday. And he wasn't trying to hide anything. Right? I mean, he even admitted to discriminating against renters. That's against the law."

Benjy nodded while KC snuck an admiring glance at her. Cat was really smart and beautiful, and he couldn't believe she was here with him. *Investigating!* His mouth drooped open watching how tenaciously she worked on this problem.

That's when Knox chimed in, "Sure she's pretty. So's the foam on a mug of suds when it's hot outside, but if you don't close your mouth and open your eyes, you won't get anywhere with her or the case, neither."

KC snapped his mouth shut and frowned. *What's eating him*, he wondered about Knox, and *why's he keep making me look deranged?*

Cat *was* looking at him, making KC squirm on the inside, but then she went on, "Guys, something's bothered me ever since I got that note. What does the writer mean, 'Give me the Piggy?'" She looked at them for answers, "What *is* the Piggy?"

Knox leaned closer to KC, "But I do see why you like her."

"Oh, come on!" he hissed back and instantly regretted it.

Cat and Benjy turned on KC slowly, frowning with worry. And annoyance. He smiled back despite knowing he'd screwed up. Again.

"C'mon... Maybe it's a piggy... bank. Like Cornelia Bank," KC chuckled and pointed at the flagship across the street. "Right over there. Biggest in town."

Cat and Benjy, though, still stared over their pursed lips like he was nuts, so he fumbled on, "If you're going to risk stealing, it's probably for something... valuable. And money's... like... bringing home the bacon, hunh?"

"Maybe," Benjy conceded more to be nice than because he believed his friend.

That 'maybe' was more like *you're crazy*, but Cat was still getting used to hanging out with them so she was willing to give KC the benefit of the doubt. "I guess it could be worth a look," she shrugged.

"Good. Great! Let's go," KC agreed and started jogging across the street before they changed their minds.

Knox hustled alongside him, "While you're struggling to impress your girl-friend, the clock keeps ticking, and you're about as warm as last night's dinner."

KC gritted his teeth, unwilling to slip into another imaginary conversation in front of his *breathing* friends. He ran ahead faster, sprinting through traffic just to get away from the pulp fiction detective. Cat and Benjy traded looks before following behind, and Knox flickered out, worry washing over his face as they ran through him to catch up.

As soon as KC reached the bank door, an older guy in a suit locked the bolt. KC knocked as Cat and Benjy joined him.

"Sorry, gang. We're closing up," the Bank Manager replied through the glass.

The kids looked at one another, then Benjy spoke up. "This might sound dumb, but we wanted to look around to make sure the bank was safe."

The Manager smiled back at them strangely. He looked carefully at each of them, and his eyes settled on KC.

"Why wouldn't we be safe?"

"We're investigating an incident at our school yesterday," Cat told him. "Has anything unusual happened here?"

The Manager unbolted the door and opened it up a crack, "Apart from the three of you showing up? No." Then he said, "You're KC Green, aren't you?"

KC sighed and nodded, "That's right."

Unexpectedly, the Manager pushed open the door wide and smiled even wider, "Your dad saved my bank the only time anyone ever tried to rob it."

KC grinned while Cat and Benjy turned to him, awestruck.

"It was an inside job, and we were scared for our lives," the Manager leaned in. "The robber made it seem like there were more of them than just him. *They* had a bomb. *They* wouldn't hurt anyone if we froze at our desks."

The Manager winced a little, remembering it, "He was smart, I'll give him that. He had it all figured out, but he didn't figure on your dad checking the back when things seemed fishy on the floor. He cornered the lone mastermind as *they* staged a getaway with an acetylene torch in one hand and a hundred-fifty thousand dollars in the other."

The Manager put a hand on KC's shoulder. "Your dad saved our entire reserve and even talked Worth into giving himself up."

KC's eyes went wide.

"Will Worth?" Cat asked. "The janitor at our school?"

The Manager snickered, "Don't ask me how he got a job with the school board. I'm the sucker who hired him here, but I didn't think anyone else would make the same mistake."

He held his hands out wide, "If you want to poke around for a few minutes, be my guest. I don't care if the Cornelia Courant thinks you're a menace, son. If you hear anything funny, you let me know. Okay?"

Stunned by this news about Will Worth, the kids nodded, dumb-struck.

"Thanks for your help, sir," KC said, too dazed to accept the man's offer. "You can lock it back up. I think we got everything we needed."

The Manager nodded and bolted the door before disappearing back inside the bank.

The kids didn't know what to say to one another until Benjy spurred them back to business, "C'mon, let's get Ms. Sosaurus' supplies before they close up the supermarket."

They trudged down the street. Knox flickered back to watch them go, but he wasn't alone. A large delivery truck slipped into drive and idled slowly after them, a half a block behind. At the wheel, a man in a hoodie wore dark sunglasses even though the sun had set. It was the stranger from the day before.

Chapter 12

Cornelia's lone supermarket, which wouldn't have seemed so super if you were from somewhere else, was mostly empty a half-hour before closing. Benjy was in the arts and crafts section, rifling through the store's posters. None was bigger than 4' x 3' and even with $50 from Miss Bridget they wouldn't have enough money to make the long banners she'd asked for.

"These will never be big enough. What do we do?" he moaned.

KC was puzzling over what they'd heard at the bank about Will and didn't answer at first. He probably should have been even more suspicious of their janitor, knowing what he now knew, but replaying the incident with the stranger on the street he was more sure than ever it had been somebody different.

One fact convinced him. Will was an ex-con who had every reason to hide from a policeman visiting their school, but instead he tried to save KC from Grist during his interrogation. Grist looked ready to kill KC, and that *had* to be why Will came in when he did. *Plus, if Will wrote the note and bumped into me on the street, why's he look me in the eye every chance he gets,* KC wondered. His gut screamed that it was because Will *didn't* do it.

"Try meat and poultry," KC finally answered Benjy.

"To what? Make them out of pork chops?"

Cat got it, though, and smiled, "Oh..."

"They've got those big rolls of butcher's paper," KC said as Benjy's eyes lit up. "Maybe they'll sell you one."

"Good idea," Benjy bounded down the aisle in that direction. "Right!"

That left KC alone with Cat.

Oh man! was all KC could think again and again, but Cat snapped him out of it by asking, "Did you know about the bank robbery?"

"Yeah," KC said as they paced through the store. "But my dad doesn't like to talk about stuff like that. So he didn't tell me it was Will. Just that there'd been trouble."

Cat *humphed* while taking that in, and KC thought out loud, "It makes sense now why Grist was so tough on Will. He must have been there after my dad caught him."

"Can I see that drawing again?" Cat asked, and KC unfolded it from his back pocket.

She looked at the uncanny likeness and poured over every detail, and even before she said anything KC knew what was coming, "He looks a LOT like your drawing."

KC nodded warily.

"Do you think it was him?" she pressed.

KC was shaking his head before she'd even finished. "Are you sure?"

"I know he looks like the guy. He looks exactly like the guy, but I also know it wasn't him." KC stopped walking near the entrance of the store and looked in her eyes. "I can't put my finger on it, but I'm sure."

"It's such a strange coincidence," Cat kept digging. She wasn't going to be convinced.

"I know it wasn't him, okay?" KC asked, though it wasn't a question, and when she opened her mouth to argue with him he tensed up. "Just because Will tried to rob a bank a bunch of years ago doesn't mean he did this," he pleaded, but she still wasn't satisfied.

Cat inched forward to debate him some more. His head started to shake, and since he didn't want to go from first words to first fight in just one day, he walked away. Down the aisle, his feet led him to the frozen food section, and leaving her behind, she looked furious.

He'd apologize to Cat, but right now he had to put the pieces together and *what lies on the surface lies.* Knox told him that a long time ago, and that idea bounced around in his cerebrum, the part of his brain that figured things out.

His eyes were clamped to the ground in front of him, and he walked on, not mad but also not going to second-guess himself. *This situation lies like a rug.* Deep down, in his gut, he knew somebody was setting their janitor up.

KC was so deep in thought, he almost stumbled on top of Detective Grist in tears, on his knees, hugging Bobby G in the freezer section and mumbling "I miss your mom."

Beside them, their trolley was full of TV dinners and garlic bread and vegetables in bags. In the white glare of all that frozen food, the mood was like a hospital waiting room.

Grist didn't see KC at first, but hearing somebody approach he shot up, wiping his nose on the back of his hand. He turned and saw KC and wrinkled up his face like somebody'd farted.

"I'm checking out, Bobby," Grist turned his back on both of them and marched off with their cart.

"Sorry," KC started to say, but Bobby's fist in his stomach took his breath away.

Doubled over and gasping, KC heard Bobby open the freezer door behind him and pull stuff off the shelf. His stomach throbbed where a hand grenade must have burst under his rib cage to knock all the air out.

Bobby ripped off KC's backpack and dropped it. KC couldn't lift his gaze above the cracks in the linoleum where a dribble of his spittle pooled. Then Bobby pushed him inside the freezer.

Back-pedaling, his feet tripping up and over the shielded fluorescent tubes inside, he stood straight as he was shoved in tight. KC was so thin, he actually fit which Bobby discovered when he shut the door on him and wedged frozen breadsticks in the handles to barricade him.

"That's for ruining everything!" Bobby growled, red-faced.

"Wha--" KC gasped with his cheek pressed against the freezing glass.

Bobby G looked so mad, for a second KC was glad to have a shield between them. When he pushed against the door and the shelf behind him, though, and realized he was stuck like a sardine in a can, the feeling passed. To top it all off, his breathing just fogged the window over, making it harder for somebody to find him.

Bobby smirked and marched off, whistling. The bars faded out of hearing, and since KC couldn't see anything beyond the frosted glass, he turned his head and found Knox Chase standing beside him by a stack of TV dinners.

"Nobody wants you to crack this case more than I do, kid. Believe me, but the immediate task is getting even."

"What about getting out of here?" KC asked, he didn't want Cat to discover him like this.

"You got into this squeeze all by yourself, and that's how you gotta get out, but let me give you a tip. After you're sprung... Keep your cool. Understand?"

KC's teeth chattered, "I'm already freezing...," he laughed without finding anything particularly funny.

"No. Listen. Mold this... moment into something you'll savor. No matter what else happens, make sure Bobby gets his *just desserts*." Knox flickered away promising, "You'll see..."

KC was shaking his head as much as he could, absolutely no idea what his friend was talking about. He would have hollered after him, but he could hear somebody sliding out the bread-rolls and tugging open the door. It was Benjy, *thank you!*

Shivering, KC stumbled forward, and Benjy rubbed his hands along KC's trembling arms, asking "What happened?"

"Bobby G," KC rasped through sharp breaths. "I saw him holding his Da--da-Dad who was crying. Bu-bub-bobby said, I ruined everything."

"Whatever that means," Benjy frowned.

"Don't tell Cat about this, okay?" KC trembled.

He didn't want her thinking he was a dweeb on top of being a freak.

"Duh," Benjy said, punching KC in the arm.

He picked up the butcher's paper he'd put down on the floor, and KC put on his backpack. Then they set off looking for Cat.

She was in jams and jellies, and one look at KC wiped all the anger and hurt off her face. Whatever she'd planned to say got erased by his blue lips and phosphorescing skin.

"What happened?"

KC looked at Benjy and shrugged before admitting, "I had a run-in with Bobby G."

"That kid..." she fumed, and her cheeks got red.

KC looked away, embarrassed, and his eye spotted dozens of red things all around them. Raspberry jam, strawberry preserves, and dozens of little red and white boxes of gelatin that made an idea pop into his head.

He smiled. *Mold this moment... Keep your cool...*

"You wanna hear something funny?" he asked her, and he turned to let Benjy in on it too. "I know how we're gonna get even with Bobby G. Deliciously."

They smiled back at him, but KC thought their smiles were the kind you'd give somebody after a lobotomy. Either way, he knew they'd be excited soon enough once he told them his plan.

"Don't worry guys, this is gonna be sweet!" he promised, laughing, and then ran off.

"Where are you going?" Benjy hollered after him.

KC didn't slow down to answer but shouted over his shoulder, "We need a shopping cart."

Chapter 13

KC hauled two overflowing shopping bags filled with gelatin boxes, and Kat toted another one, equally crammed. Benjy fidgeted, lugging the heavy roll of butcher's paper the store manager had donated once he heard what it was for.

It was only 7:30 when the kids approached their empty elementary school, but it felt much later. All of them were due home soon.

"What makes you think we'll even be able to get in?" Benjy wondered like he hoped they couldn't.

"I noticed that this door doesn't shut right when I got suspended the other day." KC pulled the side door with the propped open lock, and voila. "Shall we?"

Kat smiled and led the way inside.

Benjy lingered a little. "How long do you think this will take? I have to get home by 8."

"We'll hurry," KC promised, waving him in and following close behind him.

Inside, the hallways were a little smoky. It smelled like very old food. Greasy, kind of like when you first lit up a barbecue after a long winter. It was not what you expected to find inside a school, and they all stifled coughs.

"What is that?" Cat asked as KC led the way to the janitor's closet.

"I don't know, but we've just got to get the skeleton key Will keeps on his cart," he said.

He tried the handle to the custodial room, and the door was unlocked, so he swung it open. This closet was so black, it was like no light had ever penetrated it. The three of them hung in the doorway, silhouetted in smoky relief by the after-hours safety lamps, but Benjy reached inside the room to feel for a light-switch.

"Nothing," he gave up, his feet planted, unwilling to go any further.

No one moved until KC shuffled blindly into the room, half-steps at a time, waving his hands ahead of him. "There's got to be a draw-string," he said just as he brushed a tiny cord with a dangly weight on the bottom. "Got it!" he pulled, and the swinging fixture above clicked to life, casting a roving low-watt pallor over the tiny space.

It was maybe ten feet by twelve, and their shadows stretched and shrank, climbing up and down the walls with the motion of the yellow bulb overhead. The effect made KC a little queasy.

Will's cart rested a few feet in front of them and took up a quarter of the real estate. Coat hooks and shelves and cleaning supplies were on one side. Past the cart there was an open cabinet beside a few lockers that were shut. There didn't appear to be anything on the other side of the room, just enough space to squeeze through. A sink basin was built into the floor in the corner, but the cart mostly blocked it from view.

Benjy's eyes settled on the janitor's keys clipped to a peg on the cart. They glinted in the swinging light.

"There," he pointed, eager to leave. "Grab the keys, and let's get out of here."

KC smiled and lifted the keys off of the cart, then turned to go but Cat was heading for the lockers.

"What are you doing?" Benjy's voice quivered.

"We should search these," Cat sounded like she was trying to convince herself.

KC stepped in front of her, "We just need to borrow the keys for the locker. That's Will's property."

Knox glowed to life in the doorway behind Cat, scowling "Are you kidding me, amigo?"

KC shook his head, almost imperceptibly. *No.*

"Listen, I know you don't think it was him," Cat broke in, "And I trust you. I just want to prove it isn't so we can find out who *is* doing this."

"I don't know if it's Will Worth or not," Benjy chimed in. "But if it is, I don't want to open that locker and blow up."

KC frowned, "Forget about blowing up, we aren't going to 'prove' a thing by opening this locker other than that we snuck in here after school. My gut tells me that he's not our guy. Let's leave him be."

It wasn't easy for Cat to give in on something. KC could tell she was used to winning. Plus, he understood suspecting Will, given his background. He couldn't figure out why Knox was giving him such a hard time, though.

"There's no teacher to give you an A in manners, kid. It's up to you to dot the i's, cross the t's and chase every lead," Knox lectured.

"I thought you were the big-time investigator who wanted to get to the bottom of things?" Cat challenged KC.

"I do, but I'm not going through Will's stuff."

"Cause he's a criminal?" Benjy asked.

"No, because somebody's setting him up," KC declared.

Cat and Benjy both *ohhh'd* when he said this, but Knox asked, "Are you willing to bet your life that you're right?" KC didn't blink. "And what about your friends? You're gambling their pensions on a hunch. You get that, don'cha?"

KC gulped and then walked past Cat like the matter was settled.

Knox shook his head at him in disbelief, "The law of averages is the only one I take seriously, and I didn't teach you to risk it like this."

KC swallowed the doubt in his throat and looked back at his friends, "C'mon, let's go. Let's treat Bobby G to a taste of his own medicine..."

Benjy giggled nervously and hurried out the door. Cat stood her ground but broke into a smile, signaling that KC should take the lead. They both passed through Knox Chase, shaking his head in the doorway, and the three kids ran down the hall, laughing.

Their footsteps echoed. None of them noticed the custodial cart rumbling away from the wall, quietly on its casters, once they were gone.

Chapter 14

REVENGE IS BEST SERVED COLD...

Cat gripped Will's keys in her good hand in front of
Bobby G's blue locker. KC waited beside her in rubber
gloves with goggles borrowed from the science lab
stretched across his head. Benjy tugged a school fire
hose down the hall to join them, discovering that it just
barely reached, but it reached.

Three shopping bags overflowed with tiny boxes at
their feet, alongside two yellow buckets filled with dry
ice, billowing steam. There was the butcher's paper and
duct tape. This was the moment of truth.

Cat studied the ring of twenty-one keys, flipping past
the big brass ones and the skinny ones and the tin ones
until she found a tiny, rusted gray number that looked
small enough to fit into any locker. She slid it in the slot
on the red dial and twisted, and a latch inside the metal
front clicked. She tugged the door open, and they were
in.

The inside of Bobby's locker was a jagged collage of
cut-out girls, football players and heavy metal bumper
stickers slathered to every inch. There were books and
matchbox cars, empty milk cartons, moldy left-overs,

school supplies and Bobby's notebook. His favorite sweat-shirt hung beside little toys on strings that looked like he'd stolen them from first-graders.

"Operation Squiggle McJigglebottom?" KC checked with his friends.

Cat and Benny giggled nervously, and all three of them got to work. Cat tore strips of duct tape and stuck them over every corner and seam of the locker. Rip, stick. Rip, stick. Meanwhile, KC and Benjy popped open boxes of gelatin and tore open the baggies within. Again and again.

The butcher's paper hadn't cost them a penny, so the kids had spent almost every cent of what Miss Bridget gave them buying red gelatin. Strawberry, cranberry, watermelon, cherry, the discount brand and the fancy brand. If it was red, they bought it. Three bags with fourteen boxes a bag, each box stuffed with eight pouches of delicious red powder.

They cleaned out the supermarket and still had twenty-four cents left over. Almost enough for a gumball.

As Cat applied the final strip to seal the inside, she looked up and grinned, "She might not be a very good teacher, Benjy, but Ms. Bridget's okay with me."

Then Cat stood beside her friends, and KC handed her a flavor packet and asked, "Would you do the honors?"

Her eyebrows crinkled, "Gladly."

She poured cherry powder all over the floor of Bobby G's locker. Benjy and KC each took a turn doing the same. Then all three quickly grabbed more flavor sachets, bumping and jockeying into one another trying be the one who put the most gelatin on the rising mound of sugary sweet revenge. Envelope after envelope, they laughed hysterically while draining over 300 packets, until the pile reached almost to the sleeves of Bobby G's sweat-shirt.

Out of sweetener, KC asked the others to step back. He lowered the safety glasses over his eyes and carefully emptied the first bucket of dry ice into the locker. The pellets sizzled as they hit the powder pyramid, and pink mist fogged up instantly.

Halfway through emptying the second bucket, KC shouted, "Seal it up! Seal it up!"

The locker was threatening to spill ice and powder all over the place. Plus, he could hardly see what was happening through the cold pink volcano now pluming at his feet. Cat slammed the door in front of him and scooped up the duct tape to seal the locker's hinges while Benjy ran back to the fire hose case.

Slapping the brass water wheel, he shout-whispered "Are you ready?"

"No, hang on," KC and Cat giggled back. "Wait!"

This was it. He and Cat were shaking uncontrollably with spontaneous titters that made sealing up the last of Bobby's locker even harder to do.

When they'd finished, KC fitted the hose against the door vents and said, "Easy does it. Just a little."

Benjy gave the wheel a single twist, and water whisked the length of the hose, making it snap full. Bracing to steady it, KC nudged the pressure valve under the nozzle open, and the flow streamed into the locker and onto the dry ice. Cold pink smoke flooded out of the vents while excess rivulets spilled down all over the floor.

"We're gonna have to mop this up," Cat frowned.

"But not until we're done," KC agreed, and she smiled, nearly making him bobble the hose.

It sounded like a mini 4th of July in there. Dry ice crackled with the gelatin, and condensation formed on the sheet metal like it was a can of soda in the summer.

Benjy asked, "Is that enough?"

"What do you think?" KC turned to Cat.

"Fill her up," she advised before they both cracked up again.

They let the water come almost to the brim of the vents before telling Benjy to kill it. KC shut off the nozzle, and he looked at Cat. She beamed back at him. Inside the locker, they were making Bobby G something he so richly deserved.

"Let's wipe up the water on the door before it freezes and come back with mops for the rest," KC suggested.

Other than the duct tape holding in their frozen concoction, their sleeves wiped up all signs of what they'd done.

"After this, you want to *chill out* at my house?" Benjy asked, and the three of them cracked up in unison all over again.

They practically bounced their way back down the hall to the janitor's closet.

The air in the custodial hallway was sootier by the time they returned, and it was even thicker near the closet. The kids coughed and waved their hands to clear smoke out of the way.

"Do you think there's a fire somewhere?" Cat wheezed as they approached the closed door.

KC shrugged, "Let's grab the cleaning supplies, and then poke around to make sure everything's okay."

Benjy glanced at his vibrating cell-phone with what must have been his mom's seventh unanswered call. KC knew Benjy couldn't tell her what he was *actually* doing, and it never occurred to him to lie. So, he ducked her calls, knowing she'd call out a search party if he didn't check in quickly.

"KC," Benjy held up his phone.

"We'll hurry," and KC opened the door on the pitch black closet.

"Turn the light on," Benjy implored, but KC headed deeper inside with arms swinging on nothing but empty space as he inched ahead bit by bit. He expected to bump into the cart any second. "I can't find the string. It isn't here."

"Guys, didn't we leave the light on?" Cat asked, a chill creeping into her voice that made everyone freeze.

Then the light CLICKED on as someone else pulled the string.

The kids screamed.

Standing in front of the locker was 6 foot 1 inch Will Worth with a big smile across his lips. "It was keeping me awake," he chuckled.

In the dim light of the trembling bulb, shadows crawled beneath Will's dark eyes, and Cat and Benjy fumbled into each other, backing towards the hall. They shook so hard, though, their bodies moved in every direction except where they wanted them to go.

KC stood his ground and reached his hand over his shoulder into the back-pack he wore, quietly unzipping the top pouch.

"Hang on..." Will said, and that made Benjy turn around to run, but in his haste and terror he knocked into the closet door, accidentally slamming it shut on them.

Cat turned to face Will and braced herself, tensing her cast like a club. KC spread his feet apart for leverage while his right hand paused inside the top of his backpack, and he grasped the monoscope by the handle.

"I don't want to hurt you," he informed Will coolly, despite the terror he felt within.

"Hang on, please!" Will begged. "I'm sorry! I don't want you to hurt me, either." He got down on his knees and held his hands up above his head. "Stop! Please!"

Benjy stopped scrambling for the handle, and ironically, he found it and opened the door, but he didn't run very far through it. Cat gaped open-mouthed at KC, no idea what kind of weapon the monoscope could be as he calmly pulled it into view.

"What are you doing here?" KC asked.

"It's my job. I'm cleaning the boiler," Will laughed frantically, and then he took a breath. "It was mean of me to scare you like that. I'm sorry. But you guys *were* going to sneak through my stuff, and I wanted you to be more careful."

Cat looked down, a little ashamed, but KC said, "We talked about it, but we didn't do it."

"I know. I was sleeping on the cot behind the cart when you came in before. And I was just heading back from the boiler when I heard you coming and thought it would be funny to scare you." He looked down, "It wasn't, and I'm sorry, but here. Take a look around if you want to. It's okay."

Will gestured behind him and got back to his feet slowly to open the lockers. There was some personal stuff and a change of clothes, but even from a few feet away it was clear there was nothing suspicious.

"I keep it unlocked so everyone knows I've got nothing to hide," Will told them.

Benjy took a step closer but wouldn't leave the safety of the hallway for anything. Cat looked up guiltily and admitted there was nothing there. KC knew it didn't prove anything since Will could have moved incriminating evidence away after they'd left, but the janitor didn't seem guilty of anything other than a bad sense of humor.

"Maybe I shouldn't leave it so open since somebody made off with my clothes and broom a couple of days ago," Will remembered and turned back to the kids, "And KC, you should be more careful, too."

"How do you even know my name?" he asked. "I've never talked to you before."

"I owe your dad," Will said.

It was such a weird thing to hear after learning that KC's dad had actually captured Will Worth, that it caught all the kids by surprise.

Benjy finally asked, "You mean, the guy who arrested you?"

Will nodded, "KC, your dad saved my life. Literally, he kept Grist from shooting me, and then he helped me. I guess he believed it when I told him I was sorry, and that it was something that I couldn't get out of after I'd started. I'd spent a week wishing I could go back in time and stop this nightmare from happening."

KC didn't entirely understand, but he believed Will.

"I told him how I'd sent the fake bomb with the timer to the bank from another state and spent the 7 days in between desperate to take it back," Will explained. "I even tried to stop delivery, but I couldn't."

Will told them, "He testified at my trial about me cooperating, and that helped in sentencing, and then he got me this job when I was released. He wanted me to look out for you, KC. He thought you were getting into a little too much trouble without him."

KC smiled, pretty pleased to hear all that stuff about his dad.

"So, Mr. Worth," Cat began, but he cut her off. "Will. Please, just call me, Will."

"Will, do you know what the letter means? 'Hand over the piggy and no one gets hurt?'"

To all of their surprise, he nodded. "Yeah. It means someone's up to something. And you three have to be more careful. Not all criminals are as open-minded as me."

"Okay, yeah, thanks,' they chuckled.

"And not that I saw anything incriminating," Will changed the subject, "But I'd be happy to clean up any messes around Bobby G's locker--" They protested that they'd do it, but Will insisted, "I'm happy to clean it up since I'm stuck here tonight anyway. Besides, I want to make up for the world's worst practical joke..." he put his hand out, "So long as I can get my keys back."

Cat pulled Will Worth's key ring out of her pocket, blushing.

"Thanks!" KC told Will, as Cat tossed his keys back to him.

"Don't mention it," Will caught them. "Please. Ever."

Everybody laughed.

Chapter 15

Benjy and KC walked Cat home because her big house was close to school and on the way to their smaller houses across Memorial Square. She'd been quiet for most of the way. When they reached where she lived, the extra big front windows washed her yard in warm light.

She turned to KC and asked, "Were you scared? In the closet with Will."

Honestly, he was petrified. When Will turned up out of the darkness in that tiny room, KC's insides turned to jelly. If he'd had more to drink that day he'd probably have peed his pants.

The only thing that had gone through his mind, though, was looking out for his friends so he told her, "I just wanted to keep everybody safe."

She looked at him. Her lower lip fidgeted a little, and she swallowed and nodded, getting red in the cheeks.

"Okay, good night!" she blurted out and ran up the steps to her house, leaving KC and Benjy on the sidewalk.

They just shrugged at each other, not knowing enough about Cat to interpret her disappearing act. They walked on, hardly talking to each other, each of them swimming in his own thoughts. KC smiling and Benjy frowning.

By the time their homes glowed at the end of the street, KC noticed Benjy's expression and asked, "You worried about your mom?"

Benjy shook his head. "Not really. She told me how disappointed she was in me already, so I don't think she'll beat me up about it much more."

Benjy seemed sad by the thought he'd disappointed his mother, but KC didn't think *that* was what was bugging him. The fact that Benjy was so open with his feelings and so honest was one of the best things about his friend, but KC was routinely shocked by just how open he was.

Benjy whirled on KC. "Are you okay?"

He put extra special emphasis on *okay*, like he knew the answer was going to be no, and he wanted KC to believe he'd be there for him if it was.

"Yeah." KC felt better than okay. He felt kind of terrific.

Cat had gone from thinking he was a deranged maniac to almost thanking him for trying to protect her, if that's what her hurried goodbye was all about. Plus, they were investigating a real case. After years of play-acting, that was exciting, even if he was terrified that real people could get hurt.

"You were pretty weird today..." Benjy said, and his words hung in the air like in a comic book.

"What makes you say I was weird today?" KC asked without wanting to know the answer.

Benjy laughed like he'd just heard the least funny joke of his life, "I guess it was really the night you knocked Mr. Jenkins out of that tree, but you were evidently talking to somebody who wasn't there. That's really a problem, don't you think?"

Benjy swallowed and stopped on the sidewalk in front of his house, putting his hands on his hips and blocking the way. KC looked him in the eye but only managed to shrug in response.

Benjy pressed harder, "Mr. Jenkins actually mentioned 'Knox...' Knox Chase? He's the one you're always talking to, I guess?"

KC shook his head, eyes wide open, like he was begging his friend to stop talking, but Benjy kept on digging.

"So, how did Mr. Jenkins know about Knox, KC?"

Benjy made it sound like this was the most important question that had ever passed his lips, but KC felt differently. After everything else that had happened that day, the fact that Mr. Jenkins knew about Knox seemed about as significant as the lunch ladies running out of pizza when you were next in line.

Except now, his best-friend might as well have been accusing him of licking lit light bulbs or howling at the moon or any one of a million other crazy things, because he had to be nuts. *Right?!*

"That was kind of weird, wasn't it?" KC tried to laugh it off. *What am I supposed to say?* he wondered. That he talked to somebody who nobody else could see? That would make KC certifiably CRAZY! *Wouldn't it?*

Keeping this from his parents was easy. They never told him sensitive details about their things: who his dad was interrogating or who his mom was showing houses to or how much they were selling for. Maybe that's why they didn't dig too much into what KC was doing.

It was harder keeping it from Benjy, though, since he would gladly share the date of his last cry, the results of his worst test score or the fact that his mother was disappointed in him and how much that hurt his feelings.

"Is there something bothering you, KC, that I could help you with?" Benjy put his hand on KC's shoulder and looked him in the eyes.

KC wanted to confess about the flickering, black-and-white detective who only he could see. The advice and the stories, the chess matches Knox never let him win and even the poetry that had gotten them into this trouble. If he told Benjy about the palooka private eye who kept butting his nose in, though..., KC didn't know what would happen. *No, I can't tell him,* he decided.

KC chuckled, patting Benjy on the shoulder, "Nothing a good night's sleep can't cure. Thanks, man."

Benjy frowned. Then he sighed. Then he nodded, knowing he hadn't gotten the whole truth. It was obvious from the pug-faced disappointment scrawled across his disapproving stare. He trudged up the steps to his house like he was carrying something heavy and kept looking back at KC who just smiled at him to get on with it.

Benjy opened the front door, and his mother's guilt-trip traveled all the way to the curb, "Do you know how sad we were that you were so late?!"

Benjy dragged himself inside, and Mrs. Young glared at KC who waved back meekly. She didn't respond and left him standing there alone until Knox Chase flickered in beside him.

"Six years to sniff me out...," Knox chuckled, "You want me to take care of Benjy for you?"

"Thanks, Knox! You're the best!" KC huffed, not meaning a word of it, and he stormed away, but not before Benjy saw him arguing with no one in particular.

Knox sighed, watching Benjy stand there frozen in shadow until he eased the front door closed. Certainty and worry were tattooed across KC's friend's face.

Knox shook his head, then jogged after KC, complaining, "I'm trying to get your training wheels off for our first big case together, and it's like pearls before swine with you lately."

"You won't tell me who it is!" KC fired back as Knox caught up to him, "But you've got all kinds of helpful suggestions..., *Go through an ex-convict's locker... with him lurking in the room.* It's shocking I don't pay more attention to you, Sherlock!"

"What are you complaining about?" Knox matched KC stride for angry stride. "Since you picked up this broad, I've had better cooperation from stiffs in the morgue."

"Maybe I'm tired of having a figment of my imagination mess up my life," KC simmered over.

Knox laughed. "Figment? Now I'm just a figment? That's an awfully big word from such a tiny private eye... Detective Freud." KC scoffed, but Knox kept laying into him, "You should listen more and speak less, you'd learn a thing or two about your chosen profession."

KC stopped cold and whispered fiercely, "I didn't choose. You did. You picked me. I never picked you."

Knox unwrapped a lollipop and plopped it in his mouth, "If this is the brush off, partner, just know I always cared."

"You cared? About me? Funny, because I've read every single one of your books, and I never knew you cared about anyone. Anyone but yourself."

"Read between the lines. I care about right and wrong," Knox intoned. "When truth can't breathe for all the cash and connections heaped on top of it, I'm on the case."

KC pounced. "Great. You got any friends hiding somewhere I never got the chance to meet? Or did all of them cross you in the end? Did you ever want to get married...? No kids... No house..."

Knox smiled back without pleasure as KC asked pointedly, "Were you even happy?"

Knox took a deep breath. "I guess I wasn't written that way. You want to pick up a pencil and draw me a happy ending?" He tipped his hat to KC, "Be my guest. It'd be like Christmas every morning, but maybe it's not in my character to be... content."

"Well, maybe happy is how I want to be," KC told him and walked away.

This time Knox didn't follow, lingering where KC left him, but he shouted after his friend, "Ignorance isn't bliss, KC Green. And you won't smile if they get away with it."

KC kept going, muttering "We don't even know what *it* is!"

"Exactly," Knox flickered away into the dark night.

Chapter 16

TWO DAYS AFTER VALENTINE'S... KC MAKES A CHANGE...

When KC got out of bed the next morning, he didn't want to wear his trademark trench coat or don a fedora like he'd worn to school every single day since they moved to Cornelia. He was alone. The private eye over his shoulder was Missing In Action, and KC didn't mind one bit.

He got his teeth brushed, his face washed and his clothes on just fine all on his own. He didn't always have to dress like an undertaker, did he? So, he put on jeans, a sweater and a t-shirt underneath and traipsed down the steps to grab his ski jacket from the downstairs closet.

"Aren't you getting ready for school?" his mom snuck up on him.

"I am ready."

"Oh..." she sounded a little disappointed that he wasn't in his usual get-up.

"We're going on a field trip today," KC explained. "To visit Mr. Ringmeyer in the hospital."

"That's awful. I read about it in the paper. They have no idea who did it."

133

"Maybe Detective Grist will crack the case before your date tonight," KC oozed so sincerely, it took his mom half a second to pick up on just how sarcastic he was being.

"Okay, bud. How's about I lay off you for showing up late last night with a tale about extra-curricular activities, and you quit insinuating there's something between Charlie Grist and me? Capiche?"

"Understood," KC agreed, and he started for the door, but not before his mother grabbed him and planted a big wet kiss on his forehead.

"I miss that hat of yours, bud, but not wearing it leaves you open to all kinds of mackin' action," and she squeezed KC even tighter forcing him to wiggle his way free.

"Mom!" he laugh-shouted.

"All-right, all-right," she relented, releasing him, and he made his way out the door with a grin painted from cheek to cheek.

Outside, though, Benjy was waiting for him with a too big smile plastered across his lips, and KC wondered suspiciously, "I thought you weren't supposed to associate with me while I was working things out?"

"I'm not," Benjy agreed. "I lied to my mom and told her I was going in alone."

Benjy had never lied to anyone. *So he must really have something up his sleeve*, KC figured, but what he had was actually folded up in his back pocket.

Benjy pulled out a sheaf of papers, and he handed it to KC, "I saw you yesterday as you were leaving my house, man. Talking to your 'friend,' Knox Chase. I know you're not doing well."

KC went white. Benjy had given him a bunch of print-outs about child schizophrenia. They were from big hospitals like the Mayo Clinic, Cleveland Hospital, etc. KC knew his friend had spent hours pulling all of this together, and his eyes roamed the pages as his brain tried to conjure an explanation for last night's conversation.

A quick scan of the check-lists was pretty alarming:

• Seeing or hearing things that aren't really there (hallucinations), especially voices.

• Believing things that aren't real (delusions).

• Lack of emotion.

• Decreased personal hygiene or attention to cleanliness.

• Illogical thinking.

• Strange eating habits.

• Bad grades.

"Wha'cha reading?" came Knox's voice from over his shoulder, making KC jump.

He must have shown up when Benjy mentioned him. KC just shook his head, not just to Knox but to the evidence in his hands.

If he was honest, there were at least 2 or 3 checks against him. It really made him wonder if he *was* losing his mind. Some of this stuff, though, was just *not* him: bad hygiene, weird eating habits, bad grades and lack of emotion? *Absolutely not.*

"You haven't told anybody about this?" KC finally asked.

Benjy shook his head, "not yet, but I think my mom suspects something's up because I had to use her printer."

KC was sure Mrs. Young was already calling for men in white jackets with an oversized butterfly net, but at least Cat didn't know.

"Okay, that can't be helped, but the important thing here Benjy is I don't," and KC froze. He didn't know how to finish his own sentence.

He didn't like concealing things from Benjy, and what was worse, maybe he actually *wasn't* right in the head. Maybe talking to Knox Chase *made* him crazy. Even if it wasn't crazy to talk to him, because KC really thought he was there, maybe the guy was *driving him crazy.*

Benjy dangled there, waiting expectantly for KC to finish his sentence until he couldn't take it, "Go on..."

"I don't know how to thank you for your help," KC surrendered. "I will stop talking to Knox Chase. All-right?"

Benjy's head bobbed up and down gratefully, but Knox frowned back at him, "Figments have feelings, you know."

KC ignored him, "Even if I'm not dirty and smelly and failing school like this says I should be, maybe it's not okay for me to have an imaginary friend, especially one who's such a pain in the butt."

Knox smirked at him.

"Good," Benjy agreed, relieved that this had gone so well. "Really good."

"Good luck without me, kid." Knox said, "You'll be back before lunch."

"But you can't tell Cat about... this," KC said, waving the pamphlets at him, and Benjy wrinkled his nose and shook his head *of course not.* "Cause she'd never even talk to me if she thought I was crazy. Deal?"

Benjy took KC's hand to shake on it. "Deal."

KC glanced side-long at Knox to see how he was taking this, but the detective was suddenly filing his nails and couldn't be bothered to look up. So, Benjy and KC set off for school, and for the first time in a long time it was just the two of them.

≈≈≈≈≈≈≈≈≈≈≈≈≈≈

Ms. Sosaurus stood in front of their school with a clipboard, a tuning whistle and a furry tundra jacket next to a bright yellow mini-bus.

When Benjy and KC walked up she enthused, "All aboard, fellas! Just bring your things and hop on!"

They'd agreed to meet Cat in the school courtyard and then head to Bobby G's locker together to wait for the look on his face when he discovered the jello. Their substitute being here early was a wrinkle they hadn't planned on, and it made them wonder if Bobby G had already stumbled on what they'd cooked up for him.

Their eyes raked the bus windows where they could see half the class was already seated. Bobby G was there smiling, probably from sitting on some smaller child or farting along to a song in his head. In any event, that meant that he still hadn't opened his locker.

"Did he open it?" Cat jogged up behind them breathlessly just as Benjy and KC were about to climb up the bus steps. When both boys shook their heads with grins on their faces, she said, "Good," and then pushed past them up the stairs.

Inside, when she turned the corner, a familiar voice greeted them. "Hey, kids." It was Will from behind the wheel.

"Good morning," Cat blushed, remembering how they'd gotten better acquainted the night before.

Avoiding eye contact, she kept climbing and scouted out the inside seat on a two person bench. Behind her, Benjy slowed down once he realized Will Worth was driving.

"What are you doing here?" Benjy evidently wasn't totally reassured about their janitor.

"This trip was so short notice, they couldn't get a regular driver," Will said. "I'm helping out."

Benjy nodded and joined Cat on the bench a little glummer than he had been, but KC leapt up the steps, glad to see his new friend. "Awesome!"

From the sidewalk, Bridget watched the kids talking to Will with a puzzled expression but kept on directing the other students aboard. "This way, Reggie. I mean, Richard, sorrryyyy..." she apologized.

Behind her, Oona Pesce, the exhibit planner, strolled up to the school like she'd just foreclosed on it. She stopped long enough to smirk at Ms. Sosaurus before throwing open the front doors and sauntering inside. The kids turned to one another and shrugged, having no idea what that angry woman was up to.

Chapter 17

Cat led the class to Mr. Ringmeyer's hospital room since she knew him the best, and walking down the corridor, what she saw before she actually saw him were his legs hanging in mid-air, dangling from chains and encased in dirty, furry covers. Both his feet were in casts that extended uninterrupted to where they disappeared beneath his aqua-green hospital gown.

Cat peered around the corner and gasped as she realized the plaster didn't really end anywhere from his toes to his neck. Only his right elbow was partially exposed, and even then only until another cast wrapped around his fractured wrist. This arm dangled from its very own traction hanger, too, but at least he could sort of waggle it in something like a wave which is what he did when he saw her. His smile was equally brave and hobbled.

"Oh my gosh," Cat rushed up to him and only hesitated for a second before wrapping her arms around his chest.

His eyes, blackened from the accident and hazy from whatever medication they had him on, clouded over with a tear that he sniffled back.

He stroked her hair with his one, only slightly broken, bone and said, "There, there, I'll be dancing again in no time."

All of the other kids, including KC and Benjy, hovered by the door.

Tiny Bridget Sosaurus had to scooch and squeeze her way past them, calling "Mr. Ringmeyer, I'm Bridget Sosaurus. Don't get up!" The last bit was entirely unnecessary since in addition to the body cast, the man was in a cervical collar constraining his neck. She must have realized this when she broke through the crowd because her voice pitched even more soothingly as she enthused, "It was soooo nice of you to help the children today. They've missed you."

Then she laughed a little desperately, "We've all missed you."

Ringmeyer wrinkled up his face, gazing at her through his medicated glaze and asked, "Have we met?"

Bridget shook her head sadly, "I don't think so; but the kids talk about you so much I *feel* like I know you."

Being reminded of the kids had a sobering effect on Mr. Ringmeyer. He muffled a groan trying to shift his position to see them better. Ratcheted to the bed, he couldn't move a muscle without retweaking every one of his injuries, but he twisted his neck through a tight grimace to get a proper look at them.

The twenty-one familiar faces staring in from the doorway along with the shock of contorting, brought him back to his business-as-usual self. "Enough loitering, come in."

The kids pushed forward, more afraid of his disapproval than the state he was in.

Then Ringmeyer turned to Bridget and said, "Let's hear how they sound."

Cat positioned a straw between the fingers of his one movable appendage. He nodded and flashed her a tiny smile as she backed into the space between KC and Benjy.

"Kids...," he whisked the air with the straw as if it were his conductor's baton.

The class murmured for an instant before his glower persuaded them to begin. They belted *La la la LA* in a croaky recitation of yesterday's warm-up, just like Bridget had instructed them.

"Very funny, but time is precious. This time with intention," he insisted.

The kids glanced awkwardly at one another, and then began again in much the same way. He didn't interrupt. This time Ringmeyer didn't reprimand *them*, but instead he shifted painfully to glare at Ms. Sosaurus who giggled and shrugged her shoulders the teensiest bit back at him.

Cat smirked at Benjy. Her singing was just as beautiful as ever despite the cacophony all around.

Benjy just sang louder, regardless of key, determined to show his enthusiasm for their substitute teacher.

≈≈≈≈≈≈≈≈≈≈≈≈≈

The next two hours could have been excruciating, and without a doubt they were painful for Mr. Ringmeyer. About ten minutes into their impromptu rehearsal he dismissed a nurse trying to inject him with pain medication, insisting he'd need 'all of his faculties to repair the damage.'

Ms. Sosaurus shrank even smaller when he said this, and she was not an especially large lady to begin with.

After that, though, all the kids in the class, even Bobby G, were so moved by Mr. Ringmeyer's dedication that they focused on his every word, determined to make him feel better by doing what he said. That was the only thing that mattered.

Mr. Ringmeyer clutched the straw in his good hand until long after his fingers glowed white. He never let go, but his pained grimace gradually spread into a satisfied grin. Leading the kids in song transported him out of his hospital bed, even if just for a little while.

Two hours later their class had never sounded better. After the last pass of Mr. Ringmeyer's *a cappella* mash-up from the Mikado, Ms. Sosaurus burst into applause. "Bravo! BRAVO!!!"

Her manic gratitude was obvious, but it snapped Mr. Ringmeyer right out of his choral reverie. The rest of his complexion quickly whitened like his fingers had, and suddenly he was in dire need of that injection.

He praised them all through gritted teeth, "Wonderful... Now break a leg!" as he tensed his way back onto the pillow.

All the kids started getting their coats on, sensing their practice was over, and Ms. Sosaurus ushered them to the doorway. Cat, however, rushed back to Mr. Ringmeyer's good side and took his bare arm in her hands.

"Catarina," he smiled, "My only regret is that they won't let me attend Saturday's concert to hear you in person."

KC and Benjy, coats now on, wandered up behind Cat as she asked, "How did this happen, sir?"

He sighed, "Cupid got the better of me. I was lured from my solitude by a letter professing a certain affection and inviting me to my favorite restaurant."

The kids exchanged looks, wondering the same thing as Knox appeared, leaning beside KC's ear. "If it's not too intrusive, perhaps you could ask him who sent it?"

KC scowled. He wanted to keep his promise not to talk to Knox anymore.

Luckily, Benjy asked, "Who sent it, Mr. Ringmeyer?"

"I don't know," the teacher sighed again. "I never found out who it was."

All three kids mouthed 'anonymous' at one another, as Mr. Ringmeyer continued musing, "The note's author left, no doubt feeling that I'd snubbed the invitation. I wish I knew..."

KC couldn't help himself, "Do you have the letter? Can we see it?"

Mr. Ringmeyer pursed his lips and shook his head, not really answering, but KC pressed. "Please, sir. It would really help."

He guessed their teacher still had it.

Mr. Ringmeyer groaned, on the brink of telling them no, but he glanced in Cat's direction as she nodded, pleading wordlessly. Her knit brows and big eyes had their effect.

He blushed, "It's embarrassing..., but all-right. In the drawer, there."

Cat raced to the cabinet to fetch the letter as Ms. Sosaurus approached and put her hands on KC and Benjy's shoulders. She was wrangling them out the door to where the rest of the class waited when Cat produced the letter. She gasped.

"What is it?" Ms. Bridget froze.

Cat unfolded the note and spun it around to show the others. It was constructed from cut-out magazine letters. A charming, rhymed set of couplets inviting Mr.

Ringmeyer out for a night he'd remember at Amato's Restaurant. It was exactly the same kind of letter as the one KC had mistakenly given Cat on Valentine's Day.

"If this soup got any thicker," Knox said, "they'd serve it with a chisel."

KC didn't even hear him. He was focused with the same intensity the music teacher had demonstrated during the rehearsal.

"Did you show this to the police?" KC pointed to the letter.

"Well, there was one policeman...," Ringmeyer strained to remember his name, "most ridiculous moustache."

"Grist!" all three kids said in unison, since KC had briefed Cat and Benjy on why Cornelia needed them to crack any serious cases.

"Yes," Ringmeyer practically shouted. "*Detective* Grist. He said it was just an accident, and the driver had probably been too scared to stick around. Why?"

Benjy prodded KC in the ribs, "Show him the poster."

KC nodded and un-tucked his drawing from the back-pocket of his pants with the uncannily accurate picture of the stranger on it. Ringmeyer's eyes grew wide. He took the paper into his trembling fingers and tilted it towards him for a better look.

"It was so fast," he began, "but I'd never forget that face." Then he lifted his gaze from the page and peered at KC. "This is him, but how did you...?"

Mr. Ringmeyer panted like he was going to faint. His vital signs, which had been chirping so regularly for so long, started to ping. An alarm registered from the heart-beat gauges he was wired to, and his chest started to heave. All the kids backed away except KC.

Knox prodded him, "Get your questions answered before this guy books a one way ticket six feet under."

KC frowned, he didn't want to bother this man, but he also couldn't leave.

"Okay, gang!" Ms. Sosaurus rang out in a falsetto of fake cheer. "Mr. Ringmeyer needs his rest."

Then a nurse bustled in, brushing past them and positioning herself at Ringmeyer's bed-side. "This was too much for one day. You have to leave."

She glared at his visitors and then wheeled back around to face her patient, checking his diode connections and evaluating the levels on the monitors. Bridget practically dragged KC away, but not before he'd taken back the drawing from Mr. Ringmeyer.

"Thank you so much, sir!" Ms. Bridget bleated.

He stammered back with the nurse's fingers pressed to his neck, "Not, not at all... My pleasure."

KC, Cat and Benjy didn't say much of anything the whole walk out of the hospital. All the other kids got on the bus ahead of them. By the time they lumbered aboard at the end of the line, the only seats left were behind the driver.

The three of them squeezed onto the two-seater bench, only dimly aware of how uncomfortable it was. Bridget followed them, and Will shut the door and pulled away.

KC broke the silence, "Now there are *two* notes on top of some 'piggy' somewhere, and somebody who ran over Mr. Ringmeyer to get it."

Benjy grabbed his smart-phone and started searching for something on his browser.

Up front, Will listened in without the kids knowing.

"The ransom note writer is probably behind both notes, and we know where he lives, or at least the sidewalk he frequents," Cat said, determined to find out who did this to her friend.

"*And* what he was driving," Benjy waved his smart-phone at the others. "The Courant says Mr. Ringmeyer was hit by a green sports car."

The bus was pulling into the school driveway as Knox Chase appeared, "I never guessed your friend had so much potential..."

KC rolled his eyes at him.

"I've got a horse in this race, too, kid. So, if you think I'm leaving you alone, you're even crazier than he thinks you are," Knox gestured at Benjy.

KC ignored him and turned to the others to deliver the plan, "We stake-out the Antique Boutique; and we should also check out the restaurant from Ringmeyer's story."

"That's what I was gonna recommend," Knox grumbled.

The others nodded their agreement, but Cat added, "*After* we make sure Bobby G isn't hungry."

The three of them cracked up, but Will frowned. Knox watched the janitor closely as he pushed open the bus door using the long steel handle.

As Cat, KC and Benjy jogged down the steps, Will muttered, "Have to keep an eye on them..."

Chapter 18

Cat, Benjy and KC hustled off the bus, swinging their packs over their shoulders to clear everyone else back. Since they'd sat up front, nobody could get off ahead of them and they ran into the school giggling insanely.

Cat's flats slapped the empty hallway's tiles like a flamenco dancer's heels. Benjy and KC's sneakers smacked after her down an inside corridor to the left of the main entrance.

They flung themselves breathlessly across from Bobby G's locked locker which was still cold to the touch. KC was shaking, he was so excited, and one glance at his friends' wide eyes and manic grins told him they felt the same.

He started ripping off the duct tape from the seams, but Cat grabbed him. "What are you doing?"

"I didn't want to tip him off, and besides, it's still frozen," he smiled.

Then she and Benjy grinned and helped him strip the adhesive clean so nobody would notice anything. He took all their tape and squished it into a big gray ball that he carried to the trash as the rest of the class approached down the hall.

Since it was en route to their homeroom, everyone would have to pass this way. Cat, KC and Benjy leaned against the lockers across from Bobby's, but every time their eyes met, one of them cracked up. Then they'd all fall apart, literally leaning on top of one another to keep on their feet because they were laughing so hard.

Bobby walked up with his usual team of hangers-on, and the first thing he said was "What are you dorks looking at?"

KC kept his cool despite the nervous phlegm almost choking him, "Revenge is sweet, Bobby."

Cat glowered, all humor gone as she rubbed her cast to warn Bobby G that she was armed and dangerous. Benjy buried his head in KC's shoulder, unable to keep from losing it, he was still laughing so much.

Bobby's bushy eyebrows caved into one another, and he shook his head and turned his back on them, muttering "Losers..."

The rest of the class gathered around, 'What's going on? What's up? Why's everybody standing here?'

Wordlessly, Cat handed out spoons to her classmates. Without entirely understanding what was happening, the rest of the kids passed the utensils around so everybody got one. They knew something was up.

Bobby got the combination to his locker done but couldn't open it at first. He heaved the metal handle up, and it made a squelching wet noise. Then he tugged on the door and finally yanked it like you would if you had to rip a band-aid off of a hairy arm. A jiggling red jello universe had swallowed everything.

"Oh, man..." one kid said, and everyone else *ooooOOOH*ed.

It was huge. A solid wall consumed his matchbox cars and pencils. A baseball hat floated. His sweatshirt and treasures trembled from an invisible wind roiling everything from within. Fortunately, Cat had removed all the old food, because if not it would have hovered in mid-air, too.

Nervous laughter washed over the kids waiting to see what Bobby would do. He just stood there, though, shaking with his back to the crowd. Then his hand on the locker door started quaking so hard it sounded like a tornado tearing off a tin roof. Finally he spun around, and his face burned redder than the jello behind him.

"I'm gonna kill you guys..." he mumbled through quivering lips.

Before he could take a single step, though, Cat asked "Anyone hungry?"

The entire class surged forward, spoons in hand, and they knocked, nudged and bumped Bobby out of the way to eat. "I'm warning you, I'm gonna get you!" Bobby yelled as they jostled him aside.

KC and Benjy stepped up beside Cat.

"We'll be waiting, dingus," KC promised.

"You betcha!" Benjy seconded and then broke down in another fit of cracking up as Bobby slipped on some spilled jello and fell beneath their hungry classmates.

Devouring his misfortune, they trampled all over him, everybody crowding around as Bobby squealed from the ground, "Ow, OWH!!! Watch it!"

"That *was* pretty sweet," Cat giggled, as she led KC and Benjy down the hall, humming a tune from the Mikado.

The three of them got detention with Ms. Sosaurus for what they did, and none of them objected too strenuously. They'd already agreed to stay behind and make the over-sized posters for the concert, anyway. Besides, the kids knew they were being let off pretty easily. Mrs. Pepper kept smiling at them the rest of the day.

Making the posters wasn't even so bad. KC knew he was a good artist, but he completely blushed when Cat compared his drawing skills to her father's. Cat's dad was a really big architect who was always winning awards for the avant-garde homes he designed in North

America and the health centers he created pro bono in South America.

It turns out the Liszts had met in the middle of a Colombian Civil War when her dad was serving in the Peace Corps. Her mom was a classical music prodigy, like Cat was, but because both sets of parents opposed the wedding, Cat's mom and dad ran away to America to get married on their own.

Her mom had to support their family while her dad was in school because they didn't have any money, and that meant no more music. So now, according to Cat, her mom was more worried about Cat's ten fingers than she was about the rest of her.

"The only reason I'm allowed to be here now is because my mom thinks this is a music rehearsal," Cat confessed. Then she leaned in and looked around to make sure nobody would overhear her, "Like Ms. Sosaurus actually knows anything about music."

KC smiled warily then snuck a peek at Benjy who was suddenly bending the tip of his marker so hard it looked like the paper was bleeding. He didn't appreciate it when people made fun of Ms. Sosaurus.

"Maybe Miss Bridget needs the money, hummph?" Benjy sulked.

"Then why'd she give us $50 for these stupid posters?" Cat shot back.

Benjy put his marker down and stood up indignantly. "Because she cares about her job. That's why," then he stalked off into the hallway hollering "Miss Sosaurus, Miss, I mean Bridget!"

Cat gave KC a look, but he wouldn't betray his friend by laughing. Not when Benjy was keeping his Knox Chase condition under wraps.

He finished their Asian themed collage and got up to stretch. Stiff-legged and right hand cramped, he hobbled to the doorway where he could hear Benjy calling "Bridget, the posters are ready!"

He'd disappeared searching for her.

KC wandered over to the piano while Cat was putting caps back on all the markers. He gazed down at the instrument's keys, marveling at how she could make them ring, then he looked up from the ivories and found Knox Chase smirking at him from the other side of the baby grand.

"Rembrandt, don't you think it's time to get back to work?"

KC backed away angrily and shook his head, wondering *What will it take for Knox to get the message?* Behind him, Ms. Sosaurus poked her head in the doorway and smiled mischievously. Knox Chase saw her coming, but he pursed his lips and didn't say a word.

She glided like a ballerina on tiptoe behind KC at the piano. He turned away from Knox only to find her grinning inches from his face, and it scared the heck out of him.

"Gotcha!" She laughed, and KC leapt back, his butt squishing an opera's worth of notes as he slid across the black and whites. "What's the matter?" she teased as he knocked song sheets and a yellow book off the music stand.

Everything scattered on the floor, and KC blushed and bolted down to gather up what he'd knocked over. Cat was grinning sympathetically at him, and while crouching to avoid her worried glances, he found Ms. Sosaurus' DUMMIES Guide to Gilbert and Sullivan.

He chuckled, and she knelt before him, eyes flashing, holding out her hand. "I'll take that," she whispered icily, and Ms. Sosaurus wasn't smiling for a change.

KC was ready to hand it to her, too, but her bright red fingernails glimmering in the light made him pause. He looked at them, unsurely, then looked up at her face and saw her jaw clenching tight.

Knox Chase leaned in between them and asked KC, "You got something, finally?"

KC shook his head at Knox and then smiled to block out his interrupting. "Here," he handed over the book and promptly forgot whatever else had been on his mind.

Ms. Sosaurus snatched it, then reassembled her grin and giggled as she tucked the book out of sight.

Knox shook his head and muttered, "The cold shoulder's getting old, my friend."

Then the heavy wooden door crashed against the wall, and all heads turned to watch Detective Grist keep it from rebounding back into his face. He quivered there, angrily, mouth-breathing heavily.

"So, you'll have to enjoy this 3rd degree without me..." Knox faded out, shaking his head.

Detective Grist stormed over and pointed his finger inches from KC's nose. "Jello is serious business!" He swore, his red cheeks puffing up.

Cat and KC glanced at each other and then they both exploded, laughing. They didn't really appreciate how ticked off Detective Grist would be about his son's suffering a taste of his own medicine. *It was at least a little funny, wasn't it?*

Grist spluttered unamused, "Bobby told me about your felony vandalism, KC. It's criminal mischief, and I'm taking *you* to juvenile hall!"

Then he grabbed his handcuffs from his back pocket, and KC's giggles faded fast.

That's when Ms. Sosaurus stood up, smiling innocently. "You can't be Bobby's father. He told me his dad was a Cornelia detective, but you're way too young for that."

Grist turned in her direction, not having noticed her until then. Glancing at her up and down, though, his breath caught in his throat, and he grinned completely taken in with her. He stood up two inches higher and lowered his voice.

"Actually, I'm the Chief Detective."

KC whispered to Cat, "He's the only detective."

Grist chose to ignore KC, probably because Miss Bridget was beaming at him with full intensity. It was so much that he blushed and smiled broadly enough for all his coffee-stained teeth to glisten beneath his whiskers.

He held out his hand for her to shake, "Cornelia *Detective* Charlie Grist, at your service."

Ms. Sosaurus batted her eyes and placed her hand daintily in his, like she wanted him to kiss it. Which, astonishingly, Grist did. He looked from her watery gaze to her sweet fingers and pulled her mitt up to his fuzzy lip to plant a lingering wet one right on it.

Benjy walked in at that exact instant, and he said what was in all three kids' heads, "Ewwwwww!"

Bridget didn't notice, though, and trilled, "The pleasure's mine..., Detective."

Rather than just let Grist muscle in on the object of his affection, Benjy marched over to say, "Hang on a sec--," but Bridget talked right over him in her most enchanting tones. "Kids, would you mind giving the detective and me some privacy." Then she turned back to Grist and gushed, "I just have to learn more about you."

She was dismissing them. There was no question about it, and KC was happy to escape with his non-criminal record intact.

"Great, we'll see you tomorrow," he grabbed his bag, attracting a parting scowl from Grist.

"I'm watching you, KC Green," he growled as KC and Cat gathered Benjy's things for him.

"Then I'll be perfectly safe," KC winked before heading to the door.

Grist turned to pounce and haul him off to jail right then with Ms. Bridget's spell temporarily broken, but she latched onto his bicep and squealed the teensiest bit as she spun him back around to face her. "Is your job dangerous, detective?"

She exhaled the question in a breathy rush, and Grist looked deeply into her eyes to whisper back, "Call me, Charlie."

All memory of KC simply vanished again, which was okay with him as he carried Benjy's jacket in one arm and dragged his friend in the other. Cat brought his bag with hers, and she hustled out behind them.

Bridget giggled, "Okay. *Detective* Charlie," and they both laughed intimately, but that was the last of their conversation the kids had to hear as Cat shut the door behind her.

Benjy pouted, "Are we just going to leave her? With him?"

"Gladly," Cat answered. "Come on."

KC shrugged and followed her, but Benjy would not budge from his protest in the hall.

Chapter 19

KC and Benjy huddled beside one another inside the closed bank lobby. KC peered through the monoscope at the Antique Boutique. Benjy waited for his turn. A janitor was vacuuming behind them. Cornelia rush hour, such as it was, bustled with shoppers and cars hustling past, but there was no sign of who they were looking for.

The manager came by and gestured at his watch.

"5 more minutes?" Benjy asked

He nodded *okay* and walked back behind the counter.

"No one. Not even Mr. Jenkins," KC reported.

"We've been at this for an hour," Benjy complained. "When do we go back to check on Miss Sosaurus?"

Eyes still peeled across the street, KC smiled, "Love's for suckers, hunh?"

Benjy hauled off and punched him on the shoulder.

"Owh! That wasn't very sensitive..." KC rubbed his new bruise, bracing to defend himself against Benjy's next punch when somebody knocked on the window.

Cat was banging on the glass outside, grinning like mad.

"What did you find?" KC wanted to know, but she just waved for him to come on already, and he turned back to the Manager. "We'll take off now. Thanks again!"

The keys for the door dangled in the lock, and KC twisted them and let himself and Benjy out.

The Manager hurried over to close up after them, warning "Be careful."

They nodded without listening, and KC asked Cat again, "What did you find?"

Breathless and walk-running to where her bike leaned against KC and Benjy's in front of the bank, she gasped, "The restaurant was a wash-out. No one would confirm or deny that somebody was waiting for Ringmeyer. They didn't know."

"So what's--" KC started to ask, but she shook her head, smile gleaming.

"But I found something you've *got* to see." She grabbed her bike from on top of the pile and hollered, "Come on!" as she pedaled off.

KC picked up his own bike from on top of Benjy's. Then he punched Benjy's arm and ran off, hopping on the seat in mid-sprint, laughing.

"Owh," Benjy complained, rubbing his bicep. "That was harder than I hit you."

As the others disappeared down Main Street and Benjy rode hard to catch up, Knox frowned. He was watching the school mini-bus make a U-turn to follow them. Will Worth sat behind the wheel.

After the kids cycled down the lightly populated sidewalk at dusk, they arrived in front of Edelweiss Auto, a family-owned garage since as long as people have driven cars. Benjy and KC side-saddled their bikes to a halt and laid them down on the asphalt in front of the bay doors. Their mouths hung open. Cat mostly stifled her smile, nodding proudly at what she'd discovered.

Inside, a hunter green Jaguar with a dented front driver's side fender was mounted on a hydraulic lift. Its license plate read 'HOG HVN.'

"Hog heaven?" Benjy asked, incredulously, as the car started levitating in mid-air.

A mechanic was hoisting it for an inspection, and the kids ran inside shouting, "Wait, Stop! Hang ON!"

They didn't notice, but the school bus they'd ridden in that morning was passing slowly behind them.

At the wheel, Will leaned closer to the door to make out the license plate. He muttered, "Purcell's Pork Paradise," before driving off, unaware of Knox Chase riding in the seat behind him.

Inside the garage, KC pleaded with the mechanic, "My uncle needed me to get something out of the glove box. It'll only take a second."

Cat and Benjy gaped at him, astonished that he was lying, but he kept a straight face as the mechanic wanted to know, "What did he forget?"

"Papers... from the glove compartment. That's what he told me."

"Okay, just hurry up," the repairman huffed.

Benjy hung back by the garage's sliding doors while KC went over to the passenger side of the car and opened it up. Cat followed him closely, whispering "I thought it would be wrong to go through somebody's things?"

KC shook his head and said out of the side of his mouth, "Not if it's a lead instead of just a suspicion."

Cat frowned, unimpressed. Meanwhile, the mechanic was starting to look at *them* suspiciously, so KC cracked the glove box, dug out the registration slip and muttered the address on it to himself, "888 Oak Hill Road. 888 Oak Hill Road."

"You done?" The way the mechanic asked made it sound like KC had better be.

"Just a sec," he replied, digging beneath the Jaguar's operation manual where he grabbed a pile of Purcells' Pork Paradise flyers. "Got 'em. Thanks."

Then Cat and KC walked over to reclaim Benjy and get the heck out of there.

"What's the difference," Cat whispered as they were leaving the scene of the crime, "between a suspicion and a lead?"

"Not much," KC admitted.

She shook her head at him, and he thought it over more. "I guess the big difference is that I don't want to get into trouble if it's just a suspicion."

"And if it's a lead?" Cat asked him.

He smiled and shook his head. There was no stopping KC Green if he had a good lead.

He tucked the flyers into his backpack then all three of them got on their bikes as he repeated the address, "888 Oak Hill Road. Hog Heaven anyone?"

Benjy and Cat nodded eagerly.

"This one's *definitely* a lead," KC laughed, pedaling off into the setting sun with his friends close behind.

≈≈≈≈≈≈≈≈≈≈≈

Knox watched from behind Will as he roared down the two-lane county highway in the bus he hadn't returned yet. Trees and culverts and fields and distant mountains and a beautiful sunset and a lone bill-board for a local motor inn *'just 3 miles up ahead'* lined the road.

Knox checked the speedometer, and Will was doing close to 50 in a 35 mile per hour zone. He'd just descended a small hill that most people knew was Detective Grist's favorite speed trap. Evidently, Will hadn't driven in so long he didn't realize, and the mini-bus roared past the unmarked police car hiding behind the sign.

Knox flickered out of the bus to reappear beside the police sedan and look in on Grist 'hard at work.' He was sleeping with his feet on the dash-board and a cup of convenience store soda in between his thighs. When the school bus roared past, the detective shifted one of his legs up which titled the cup straight into his lap. Ice and freezing cola doused the seam of his pants, and the Cornelia detective lurched out of his seat, shivering.

He shook off the cold as the bus's taillights receded into the distance, and the LEDs of the radar gun blinked 51, 51, 51 in red. "Son of a buck," he trembled. "What have we here?"

He tossed the soda cup out the window, flipped a switch to turn on his police globe and peeled out of the deep rut his car was in from hundreds of traffic stops. Shooting pebbles and dust behind him, Grist raced into the distance while Knox lingered, shaking his head and sighing.

Chapter 20

CLOSE CALL...

The country road crested at the top of a small hill in the blue twilight. With its close-hanging trees and flittering pigeons shaking the branches, everything looked washed out from the short day, barely past.

The kids heaved and gasped up the opposite side of the incline, and KC chugged triumphantly over the brim first, insisting "I told you we could bike here," but an awful stench invaded his open mouth, and he wrinkled his nose and turned his face away from the invisible reek. Cat arrived close behind him, and that same stink enfolded her, making her eyes water. Ben turned up last and his shallow breaths tore at the air, desperate for oxygen but fighting not to breathe the smell in.

"Yuk, who died?" His face contorted.

"Your breakfast, C'mon," KC hopped off his bike and stowed it beside the worn asphalt.

The others followed suit, and the three of them jogged down the slope towards the grunting hogs ahead. A bright red barn with a small pigpen in front of it stood off in the distance. A farm house rose opposite the sty on the other side of the little valley, completing the picture from the flyers in the glove box.

The kids hid beside the sty with a dozen pigs running around inside.

"There's no way *these* hogs made all this stink around here," Benjy crouched near one pig who sniffed at him through the slats.

KC, Cat and Benjy were getting used to the animals' smell, but the animals weren't so sure about the kids yet.

"This is probably the Potemkin pig-sty," KC joked.

The others looked at him blankly.

It was in a history book Knox had made him read. Knox was always *improving* KC, which was why he played chess and knew poets like Coleridge and Blake, but he had no idea who the 'celebrities' on the covers of the supermarket magazines were.

"It means it's a false-front designed to fool people into believing that everything on the other side is just as beautiful as here," KC explained.

Benjy rolled his eyes, but Cat was smiling so he went on. "The Russians did it to deceive Catherine the Great by building a village called Potemkin near the Black Sea so she'd think her bureaucrats were doing a great job. The big industrial pens must be down the valley, out of sight of the road," KC guessed, and Cat nodded at him, making him smile.

There weren't any cars apart from a pick-up truck by the house up the hillside. For such a big place they had to have more vehicles than that, and KC figured the bright red barn with the big bay doors could double as a garage.

"They're kind of cute," Cat turned to the pen to watch the mother sow corral her grunting piglets.

"Yeah," Benjy replied, "I'll never eat bacon again. Where to, man?"

"C'mon," KC pointed at the barn. "That's probably it."

Not sure if the kids were trespassing or just unannounced, KC had the impression that the big house was looking down at them. Like it was an owl perched high in a tree, and he was a mouse dashing through the un-cut grass for safety, he shuffled double-quick over the fifty yards from the edge of the pen and pressed himself against the barn's rough slats to catch his breath.

Benjy and Cat were right behind, and without words they agreed to remain absolutely silent. He didn't want to open his mouth again until his heart slowed down. It was beating so loud he'd have sworn Cat and Benjy could hear it, but maybe they were listening to their own pulses pound in their ears.

Something was in the air, and he wasn't the only one who could feel it.

Benjy grinned insanely, like they'd just gotten away with something, and Cat was biting her lip. "Do you think there's even anything here?" she whispered, sounding anxious to turn around and bolt in the opposite direction.

"The only way to know something," KC quoted Knox Chase unconsciously, "is to find out for yourself."

He pointed to a high window down the barn from them and marched toward it. Unfortunately, he misjudged how easy it would be to look inside. The base of that window was two feet over KC's head, which he only realized once he'd descended the slight hill to get there. Since Cat and Benjy were watching him, though, he leapt up to grab hold.

His fingers barely caught the ledge. It was an inch thin and almost impossible to grip. He bicycle kicked his feet against the wall over and over, desperate to boost himself up, but his fingertips were burning. Dangling with no leverage to pull from, KC fell backwards from seven feet, still running up the side, which made him flip up higher into the air before smacking his back onto the ground.

Benjy giggled at him, "I'm sorry, man."

KC wheezed back as quietly as he could, not wanting everyone to know he couldn't breathe since he'd completely knocked all the wind out of himself.

"It's not *at* you. I'm just..." Benjy kept shaking his head, but KC scrambled to his feet, nodding, because he still couldn't say a word.

Cat walked over and said, "I'll give you a boost."

Benjy stopped laughing, and KC went white.

He didn't want *Cat* to give him a boost, but he couldn't tell her that he didn't want a girl to pick him up. He couldn't even speak yet, because the air wasn't going into his lungs. So, all he could do was shake his head, vigorously, but she ignored him, wrapping her right arm around his waist and her cast under his butt. Then she knelt down and pressed her face into his belly button before hoisting him up in one fluid motion.

Wow. She was a couple of inches taller than KC and obviously a lot stronger. She backed her way to the side of the barn as he finally found his voice, "But what about your arm?"

She smiled up at him and gasped, "No problem," though the act of not concentrating made her sway a step, and KC wobbled up in the air like a jack-in-the-box, but she steadied her feet and back-pedaled him to the ledge where he leaned his face against the double-paned glass.

He fogged up the window as his mouth dropped open.

"What do you see?" Cat tried not to sound like she was straining.

A yellow Ferrari, a black Lamborghini, an old 50s Corvette Stingray, a Model T Ford, a GTO and more and more. There were more *amazing* cars here than you could find in a museum, and the place sparkled. Fancy spot lights hung from the two-story high ceiling, and even though those were turned off, the mammoth space was out-fitted with utility fluorescents that bathed the hall in dim back-light, glowing off of every polished fender and shiny piece of chrome.

"It's probably two million dollars worth of old cars!" KC whispered back, astonished. "Fifteen with room for more."

Benjy marveled, "Maybe he steals things to pay for the cars. Or maybe the *cars* are stolen! And he hides them on a stinky hog farm where no one would poke around."

KC was still up in Cat's arms, and he could feel her muscles shaking against his hips, but he wanted to take in everything he could. There was a mechanics creeper, like a four-sided skateboard with cushions for sliding under cars, and a stainless steel work bench on wheels near the front doors. A pair of dark blue coveralls hung carelessly on top of it.

"How you doing up there?" Cat's voice wavered with all the weight she was holding.

"Hold on!" KC whispered intently back.

He focused closer on the clothes on the work bench, and he read out the letters W-I- and what looked like an L from a bright red name tag stitched on the front.

"Will's clothes are there. It's his school uniform," KC reported.

"Why would the hog farmer steal Will's clothes..." Benjy wondered, "*Unless* the farmer was trying to set him up. Son of a gun!"

Cat was buckling, so KC tapped her shoulder to let him down. He landed in her arms inches from her, and she smiled at him, red-faced and beaming.

"Thanks," KC said.

They blushed in unison and looked away in different directions. Then KC headed for the barn's front doors telling them, "You guys wait here. I'm going in," but Cat grabbed him and spun him back around.

Her smile evaporated. "No. If you're going, we'll go with you." Then she turned to Benjy, "Right?"

"Ugh, because you're assuming the homicidal maniac has a sense of humor?" Benjy asked, his more risk-averse side asserting itself.

Cat glowered at him, and he nodded okay. KC smiled at them and led the way.

The barn's old sliding doors were unlocked and fitted to a shiny iron track. KC braced himself to really yank them open, prepared to run if they made noise, but the twenty foot tall doors slid effortlessly. Behind them, hollow metal holes were buried in the concrete floor every six inches. These divots were a mystery, but KC didn't think much more about them.

The inside had been completely remade since the days this barn housed actual horses instead of so much horsepower. Polished fenders and gleaming bumpers glowed everywhere you looked, and the concrete floors had been poured with a glistening emulsion that defied oil to stain a single inch. Walls built on either side of the entrance formed a twelve foot wide driveway to so many fantasy cars shimmering up ahead.

KC turned to his co-conspirators beside the doors and whispered, "We don't want anyone to hear us."

The others nodded. Everyone's breaths raced, and KC's lips crept into a grin with the thrill of unraveling this mystery. Then he stepped onto the showroom floor.

A deafening alarm sounded.

Red and white security globes KC hadn't noticed before flashed to life. He looked down where his foot had crossed a previously invisible security laser that now pulsed red. Even worse, enormous chains rumbled loudly overhead.

"Look!" Cat hollered.

She pointed to a medieval-looking iron gate tumbling closed behind them. It had pointy spikes on the bottom to cage them in. Benjy went green in the red light, like he was about to lose three years of lunch, and it was almost too much for KC to process.

An iron trap closing in, ensnaring them with the man who'd run over Mr. Ringmeyer? *My investigation getting Cat and Benjy in trouble?* These questions ricocheted around KC's brain along with the siren still blaring, until he remembered the rolling mechanic's tool bench with Will's coveralls, just ahead.

He heaved it in the direction of the gate. It hurtled along the smooth concrete, wheels spinning towards the collapsing iron wall until the workbench reached the divots in the floor, and the spikes tore into it.

A screech of iron versus steel pierced all of their ears. The glistening metal tips looked like they might sheer all the way through the case, but the massive gate slowed down as the toolkit crumpled and folded in on itself beneath the two ton weight. The deadly sharp points creaked to a halt eighteen inches above the floor. Still poised to impale anything in its path, at least the wall wasn't moving anymore.

"Get Out! NOW!" KC turned to his friends.

His shout broke through the security ruckus and snapped Cat and Benjy back to life.

First Cat rolled past the spikes, her shoulder nearly brushing a metal tip as she tucked underneath. Then Benjy inched less gracefully by the points, freezing for half-a-second under a blade that would have sliced between his eyes if it slipped with him beneath it.

"C'mon," Cat roused him, and Benjy got moving again.

Then it was KC's turn, but just as he was about to head under the gate, the toolkit crumpled loudly. Folding into itself like paper smushed into a solid steel ball, what had been eighteen inches of clearance was now fourteen and shrinking. KC didn't want to be forked by those spikes if the wall kept falling with him anywhere near it.

He took off his backpack and slid it underneath, onto the grass outside. Then he ran back into the garage as his friends hollered after him.

"KC, what are you doing?!"

He picked up the mechanic's creeper and ran towards the gap between the gate and the floor. Then KC flopped his belly on top of the rig, like hopping onto a boogie board. He sailed along the smooth concrete toward the trembling spikes, crouching small and closing his eyes as he approached the razor sharp points.

Racing past them for the grass outside, he didn't look again until the creeper passed the metal and reached the lawn, dumping him safely into the field beyond. The world was spinning and every inch of KC shook so hard his bones wanted to break, but he was okay.

Chapter 21

Cat and Benjy helped KC to his feet outside of the garage, and they stood watching the gate quiver on top of the toolkit, waiting for it to collapse. The workbench held, though, and all three kids exhaled, laughing like the worst had passed.

Then a screen door back at the house slammed closed like an explosion. They jumped and turned, and from where the kids were standing it *sounded* like a shotgun blast.

In the gathering darkness, they didn't know where to hide, and all three of them locked eyes on where they'd come from, the pig-sty in the middle of the field. Benjy bolted first. Arms akimbo and running like an Olympic sprinter chased by a rhinoceros, he glanced under the house's porch light where he glimpsed a man cradling a long, dark piece of metal in his hands.

Benjy approached the pig pen at full speed, too out of breath to make for the trees and too afraid to just stand there, so he leaped over the fence. Hopping the wooden rail without stopping, he landed face-first in slop, and made pigs squeal off in every direction.

Cat and KC followed right behind but managed to land on their feet, until scrambling piglets and angry hogs charged them into the corner. The grown-up animals bucked and bumped the kids to defend their young, and KC, Cat and Benjy stumbled over one another into fresh poop and slimy earth. It suction cupped to their hands, faces, backs and fronts, slathering them all over, as they rolled behind the wall to hide from the man on the porch and escape the rampaging pigs.

Bob Purcell, the owner of Purcell's Pork Paradise, was a large, round man who waddled towards the pen with a branding iron, not a shotgun.

He muttered, "Awh heck!" with more concern than anger and wanted to know, "Is everyone okay?"

His question made the kids stop flailing, and even the pigs calmed down hearing the farmer's voice. One by one, KC, Cat and Benjy gulped and nodded in his direction as they got slowly to their feet. KC even thought *things might still work out.*

"Good. Now can anyone tell me what's--" but before Purcell could finish the question, a four-door sedan with a police globe flashing on the roof roared over the hill to the farm.

The car achieved lift-off, and the old suspension cracked loudly when it smacked back down to Earth. It burst into the driveway, skidding up a dust storm, and Detective Grist leapt into view from the driver's seat, forward-rolling with his weapon drawn as he screamed.

"Freeze!"

It scared the bejeezus out of Purcell and the kids.

"Ho-Ly," the pig-farmer muttered, and he dropped his branding iron.

It took a terrifying moment to assure the detective that *nothing* was wrong.

Eventually he lowered his side-arm, and the kids got to put their hands down and even climb out of the pig pen, which took some doing and a little help from Mr. Purcell who insisted all the while, "Shoot, detective. I only built the security system after somebody stole my car. I didn't think *kids* could have been hurt. I'm sorry, you three."

Mr. Purcell seemed like a very nice and understanding man, not at all the type who'd have run down a music teacher. Still, they'd followed a good lead to his farm, landing in pig poop in the process. KC hoped he'd some have answers, and he knew they were at a dead-end if he didn't.

He found himself wishing for Knox Chase at just that instant, even if the pulp fiction detective asked way more questions than he ever cleared up. Almost like he was listening in, he flickered into being, holding his nose but not concealing a grin.

"Looks like you didn't just step in it, my friend," Knox opined. "You dove in. But good for you. You got your hands dirty... along with the rest of you. Detecting is a messy job."

KC rolled his eyes, but he was glad to have company.

Purcell excused himself to head to the barn and deactivate the alarm which was still ringing. KC turned his focus to Grist who was surveying the three of them dripping in doody and mud.

He snickered, "No lead too stinky for you, Detective Green? And how about you two?" he turned to Benjy and Cat. "Do your parents know where you are?"

They looked down, ashamed.

"What were you even doing here?" KC challenged Grist. "Were you waiting for us? And what happened to your pants?"

The detective's slacks were stained right below the waist in a place likely to raise questions about his self-control, and this wiped the smile off of Charlie Grist's face.

"I had an accident--" Grist said, and the kids giggled. "It's just soda. An accident with a soda cup, when I was apprehending your accomplice for stealing a school bus."

The three of them had no idea what Grist was talking about, but Knox leaned in to warn KC, "If you thought things stank before, hang in there, cause there's more."

Behind Grist, locked in the back of his car, Will was suddenly visible in the headlights of a deputy pulling into the yard.

He poked his head through a crack in the window and shouted, "I didn't steal the bus. I was following you three in town when you found the Hog Heaven car. I figured--"

"Quiet!" Grist cut Will off, signaling to two deputies to bring him over.

Still cuffed, with his hands behind him, Will was led by the armpits to stand beside Grist. In the distance, the alarm from the barn stopped blaring.

"Now, what are you three doing here?" Grist demanded.

"We're doing your job!" KC shouted back.

Knox warned his friend, "If this was a paint by numbers, this stiff couldn't reach two without using both hands. Don't do his algebra for him."

KC couldn't stop himself, though, and demanded "Wake up and smell the bacon, Detective. Mr. Purcell's car hit Ringmeyer. And Ringmeyer was only there cause of a note -- anonymously cut up with magazine letters -- Just like the one I got which said, 'Give me the piggy, and no one gets hurt!'"

"So?"

Impossibly, Grist didn't seem to understand.

"We're on a hog farm..." KC scoffed.

Grist frowned and looked around, still not getting that something bigger was going on. Purcell scurried down the hill towards the group, carrying something.

"Look around, son!" The Farmer chuckled, opening his arms wide while grasping the bunched-up coveralls from the rolling bench. "I'm already up to my neck in slop. What would I need with more swine? All I know is somebody stole my Jaguar when I took the missus to town for Valentine's. Reported it, then I found these under the front seat when the car turned up."

He unfurled the Roosevelt Elementary School uniform, and Grist's eyes went wide. They were Will's coveralls, and it was as if you could hear the rusty gears in the Detective's head cranking to life. He looked from the embroidered name to the man in hand-cuffs beside him.

Will inhaled deeply, and his skin paled as all the blood drained out of his face. KC shook his head, mouth open wide.

"Those are..." Will mumbled, "They were taken from my locker."

"Hold on a minute," KC pleaded.

"I TOLD YOU MY THINGS WERE MISSING--" Will shouted, but a lop-sided grin overtaking Grist's expression made his intentions obvious.

The deputies holding Will secured him tighter, and Grist nodded at them.

They spun the janitor back around to drag him to a patrol car, all the while, Will was desperately explaining, "when you came to the school... I told you!"

"He's innocent!" Cat insisted.

Grist ignored her and turned to KC, whispering, "Can't do my job, hunh? Maybe *this* makes us even."

Then he jogged up beside Will as the Deputies were walking him back to the car. "William Worth, you are under arrest for attempted murder."

Benjy shouted, "No!"

KC's head wouldn't stop shaking, and he closed his eyes. *What does that even mean, 'makes us even?'* He fell to his knees, trembling, tears coursing down his face. *Is Grist doing this because of me? Is it my fault?*

Knox leaned in, worried, except the detective's signal seemed to be short-circuiting. Instead of words, a garbled wash of static streamed from his moving lips. He blinked in and out of existence, like electrical wires were crossed somewhere, and KC pondered what was going on. Eyes still closed. Unaware.

KC knew Grist didn't like him, but was he really going to arrest an innocent man to get back at him? For something KC didn't even understand?

And I'm helpless to stop him. Resigned hopelessness flooded KC like never before. He was young. He was small. He was sure that there was nothing he could do.

Knox Chase burst into a million sparkles, like a light bulb exploding, and the flash made KC open his eyes to witness the famous Detective on the Case, disappearing.

Maybe forever. The only trace that he'd ever existed was the after-glow burning in his young friend's retinas.

He couldn't even cry, anymore. He couldn't fight back. KC felt like a tube of toothpaste that's been wrung out of every last drop.

He slumped on the ground, on his knees, out of tears, just gasping instead of breathing. Cat rushed over to him and threw her arms around him while Benjy glared at Grist reading Will his rights.

The janitor looked back numbly, staring at everyone as if from a distance or a dream. Almost sleep-walking, he was led back into the car. The deputies kept his head from banging against the door frame, gently helping since Will's legs were buckling.

"Do you understand these rights as I've read them to you?" Grist asked gleefully. "Hey, stick with me."

Grist shook Will who looked back and nodded, his face caving in with disbelief. Then the detective slammed the door on him.

"Now for the three of you..." he turned around to stare down the kids.

Benjy gulped "Where are you taking us?"

Grist took out his cuffs and slapped them around KC's unprotesting wrists. "The end of the line," he smiled.

Chapter 22

BUSTED...?

In the bus through town, the kids were each seated on their own bench and instructed not to speak. They weren't told where they were going, and Grist drove slowly past the police station, making them think he was going to book them on trumped up charges and make them spend the night in jail. After he drove past town hall without stopping, though, it became obvious his plan was to scare them and then take them home.

KC had no idea what his friends' parents would do to them. Of course, they were all covered in the worst kind of slop imaginable. Thick, viscous mud and worse dripped off their bodies onto the floor and coated the green vinyl of the school bus seats. Now that the janitor had been arrested for something he didn't do, KC wondered who would clean it all up.

≈≈≈≈≈≈≈≈≈≈≈≈≈≈≈≈≈

    Knox released the cold metal
    handle, tiptoed behind the opening
    door and pirouetted his back up
    against the cinder blocks to hide.

Pressed between the wall and the
sticky blue walnut, a thick German
accent drilled into his ear before
anyone appeared.

"Nossing funny," the former soldier
said. You could hear the goose-
step in his voice. Heinrich or
Jürgen or whoever this Aryan was,
he had been an officer giving
orders and not just following them
in the Third Reich.

Knox knew everything that was about to happen to him,
but he had to go through with it anyway. For example,
there wasn't a doubt in his mind that he was about to
take a whack to the back of his head while saving this
woman. The only thing he didn't know was where KC
was now.

Dorothy slow danced into view
through the door frame in front of
a Mauser in this Hun's left hand.
A bruise was already darkening the
blood vessels beneath her right
eye. Her pale pink skin would be
black and blue in thirty minutes
and resemble the gun clip in the
pistol butt for a week or two. If
she lived that long.

She saw Knox. It was an eyelash wink, a fraction of a second through the crack in the door. Their gazes met, but otherwise she didn't miss a step. She looked straight ahead like she had a date with a manicure instead of marching to certain death at the barrel of a gun.

If diamonds sparkle from the accumulated pressure of millennia bearing down on them, then this lady was a rare gem. On the wrong end of a muzzle, she seemed as unconcerned as if the fly in her soup was still swimming. The only things Knox could see in her were looks and savvy, and he didn't know which was more dangerous.

Knox had been up against this hallway and this Nazi and this dame millions of times in the hands of just as many readers. They always turned the pages, breathless to see what happened next.

The German behind her was former SS like he'd just arrived from central casting. Salty blond with eyes like cloudy skies, he was over 6 feet and unbowed despite his

```
Führer's defeat.  What he was doing
here instead of warming a cell at
Nuremberg was a question for Hoover
and his G-men, but he'd seen Jän or
Helmund before.  It's hard to
forget a face like his with the
sunken cheeks and half-dead stare.
```

Knox finally had a glimpse of how *they* felt, those readers. He had to get back to what was happening with his friend, only *nobody* knew how KC's story was gonna end, and Knox didn't like his only clue.

The kid would break if Knox didn't get back there to give it to him straight. That's what drove him crazy, stuck to these pages. Knox owed KC the facts about right and wrong and all the distractions in between which seemed like good reasons for doing nothing. He'd fight to find KC, but Knox couldn't even save himself from what was about to happen.

≈≈≈≈≈≈≈≈≈≈≈≈

The bus pulled up in front of KC's house first. Grist worked the door open and then tossed KC's bike onto the lawn.

As it clattered to the grass, he walked behind KC's seat, pulled out his billy club and prodded him with it. "C'mon. Let's go see your mom."

It was like walking the plank, inching down the aisle toward the steps. KC clutched his backpack ahead of him. It was the only thing not covered in porcine poo.

Grist leaned beside KC and whispered, "You want to hear something funny?"

Grist was grinning, and KC didn't answer him. Didn't nod or shake his head, he just kept trudging forward with the detective shuffling behind him.

"The last time you meddled on a case of mine, the suspect you ID'd was my wife's brother. That's why she left me."

He's blaming me for his divorce? KC didn't think this could get any weirder.

Grist laughed strangely, though, and shrugged his shoulders, "It cost me my marriage, but I got a promotion out of it. Now with Chief Williamson retiring, I bet I'll replace him. And I owe it all to you."

KC stared at Grist as he laughed, "I was going to take your Mom out to get even with you, but now I may be spoken for..."

KC caught his breath at the top of the steps. It was hard enough keeping his balance with his hands bound before him, without remembering that his mom had planned to go out with this louse tonight.

Almost on cue the front door of his house opened, and Mary Green came out wearing jeans and a t-shirt. KC was glad she hadn't gotten all dressed up, but she was chuckling about the bright yellow mini-bus with no idea what was really happening.

"Charlie, when you take a girl to dinner, you--," but she stopped as soon as KC emerged, filthy and in hand-cuffs, in front of Grist's billy club.

He was nudging her son down the steps, explaining "Mary--"

She ran over to KC. "Are you okay?" she panted.

He nodded, and she rounded on the detective. "You take those hand-cuffs off my son right now or so help me, Charlie Grist."

He didn't move fast enough. Instead, he put his hands on his hips saying, "They're for his own protection, and as for--"

She slapped him hard across the cheek.

He must have seen sparks or something, because he had to shake the hit out of his face before turning angrily on Mary. "I could arrest you--" he started to say, but this time she slapped him even harder, spinning the detective's whole head around several inches.

A red outline of her fingers tattooed his cheek.

"Now!" she stood her ground.

Grist shook, enraged, but got his keys out to unlock KC's cuffs.

Cat and Benjy were pressed against the windows, watching, but KC could have been seeing all this happen on TV for all the affect it had on him. He was cold, and he was sad, and worst of all he couldn't believe what was happening.

Will's whole life is being reduced to collateral damage in some stupid scheme to get even. With me! At least he knew what Grist was up to, and if he could just figure out who was actually responsible for all of this trouble, maybe he could still fix it and get Will out.

There was a tiny flickering glimmer of Knox Chase by his side, almost too dark and distant to make out. KC didn't notice him, though. He'd turned back to smile at his friends on the bus, and through the mud and muck covering them, they both breathed easier.

Grist was fumbling with the lock, working hard not to get any of KC's slop on him. "I won't be able to, to make our date tonight, Mary. I hope you understand. I've made other plans."

Mary pounced as she pulled out her cell phone and held down a button, "It was a mercy dinner you forced on me, Charlie, and I couldn't care less if you're throwing out the first pitch at Yankee stadium. You tell me why you pulled up here with my son IN SHACKLES!"

Grist unfastened the cuffs and walked over to explain, but she held up her hand, cutting him off. "Ron, IT'S ALWAYS A BAD TIME. We can't wait for a good time to raise our son!" She hit the speaker button and held her cell phone beside KC's ear. "You tell him what happened!" Then she turned back on Grist, "Who do you think you are, Charlie?!"

"Dad?" KC said loud enough to be heard on the phone.

"Hey, Bud," Ron Green spoke low and close to the microphone to avoid being overheard. "I got a tip to raid the jewelry ring head-quarters. We're about to break down the door. What's happening?" Then KC heard him whisper "Johnson, Wills" to two agents who must have been nearby.

KC broke the news to him, "Grist just arrested Will Worth--"

Ron Green almost shouted "What?!" and then he whispered "Sorry," to the other guys before asking KC, "What did he arrest him for?"

KC rattled off what happened while keeping watch on his mom and Grist, "It's a set-up. We were investigating the piggy note and went to Purcell's farm to see if he ran over our teacher, Mr. Ringmeyer."

"Wait. Will Worth and Bob Purcells ran over your teacher?"

KC took a breath and tried to set the record straight, "No, the Piggy Note guy ran over our teacher; but he's framing Will. Grist is just doing this to get back at me."

Out of the corner of KC's eye, he could see Grist giving his mother a lop-sided version of things as she shouted, "The gate nearly killed KC?!"

Grist nodded, "That's why Purcell's not filing charges."

In KC's ear, his father was getting the gist of it, "Just a second-- Somebody ran over your teacher? And that's the person who gave you this note? And you're *looking* for them? You're 11 years old, and if you want to see 12 you'll stop this right now!"

KC pleaded, "Dad! Will's innocent, and he's in jail because of me. We have to crack this case before--," but Ron talked over him.

"KC! You're a kid. You can't be held responsible--," but whatever else his Dad was about to say died on the line as Mary spun the phone back around.

"Ron, this isn't working," she insisted, red-faced. Then she swallowed and glanced at KC before walking away.

He got all tingly. From the tip of his nose to his fingers and toes, an awful premonition came over him, and he started shaking his head at her, but she wasn't looking.

Mary whispered just too loudly into the phone, "Ron, if I'm going to do this all alone, I want a divorce."

KC's heart stopped beating. *This* was his fault. It was happening for getting in trouble. For sticking his nose where it didn't belong. He interfered with *everything*, and now his mom was leaving his dad and Will was going to jail.

He looked up. Grist was grinning at him. It was a stupid, mean smile, but KC couldn't turn away. He wanted to hurt for what he'd done to his family.

The detective's lips puckered as he broke off from glaring to glance at his watch. Then he tried to get Mary's attention.

"No, no, you're not a bad influence," she reasoned with her husband. "You're no influence at all. You aren't here, and KC needs someone who is.-- What?" She huffed at Grist.

"Somebody's waiting for me. Big date..." He tapped his toes excitedly.

She inspected him up and down before recommending, "Well, change your pants first."

Grist's smile wilted, and he wanted to explain how he'd wet his trousers in the line of duty, but she cut him off with another raised hand and went on listening to her husband plead on the other end of the line.

"I don't either, bud," She fought unsuccessfully to keep the tears out of her voice. "I love you, but, Good-Bye," and she hung up the call.

KC snapped out of his funk enough to run for the house and not look back, no matter who was calling for him to stop. Even if it was Knox shouting with everything he had left. The pulp fiction detective frowned and watched him go before disappearing into the night.

Chapter 23

Knox Chase flickered into a low-rent apartment building hallway, but his hazy signal fuzzed with static. Ron Green stood beside him, frozen, with a long dead cell-phone still pressed to his ear. He shivered in the sweltering corridor, and his eyes focused somewhere that was nowhere near.

FBI SWAT agents surrounded KC's Dad, watching and waiting for him to give the sign. They held a battering ram and shot-guns and wore bullet-proof vests and baseball hats turned backwards, all staring at him.

Finally, Ron breathed deeply and shook off the cold. "All-right. Now."

The FBI team charged with barely a sound. Ron holstered his phone and pulled his side arm to catch up. The jingling of metal on their utility belts and the clank of the steel tube roaring down the hall were all you could hear until the collider splintered the flimsy wooden door.

Ron shouted, "Freeze, FBI!" and he barged through the fragments into the apartment first, weapon leveled and advancing two steps.

Then he paused by a small table, as the other agents fanned out in both directions around him to scour the deserted apartment, hollering "Clear, clear, clear."

Ron frowned and picked up a folded piece of paper addressed to, "Special Agent Green" in cut-out letters.

Knox's frequency wavered. He watched him unfold the note of more clipped characters which read, "Sorry you missed me, Ron, but I'll see YOU soon!"

≈≈≈≈≈≈≈≈≈≈≈

The bathroom had a door lock, and KC's mom could knock and knock but he didn't have to let her in. He didn't want to look at her or hear her, and he stayed under the showerhead long enough for the hot water to turn cold and the knocking to stop. Then he toweled himself off and listened at the doorway for any telltale signs of Mary Green planning to ambush him on the other side. He put on his robe and made a break for his own room.

Leaning against the other side of his closed door, he didn't want to remember that his folks were getting divorced, so he went through everything that had happened to force his brain away from his parents. He pictured the stranger, the bank manager, Mr. Ringmeyer, Will Worth being led back to the patrol car in handcuffs. Nothing helped. *He had to keep his Mom and Dad together*, but he didn't know how.

He opened his eyes. Knox Chase flickered back before him, barely. His image was grainy and too bright and suddenly gone and then back again, pulsing like an erratic heart, beating its last beats. Knox was disappearing. *There's nothing I can do*, KC brooded and the flicker went out.

"Knox," KC called in a fervent whisper, and he barely summoned the image of the detective back. "I need you. What can I do?"

Knox glowed stronger and surer and brighter for an instant. "No. I need you," he called from far away. Surprise crept into KC's face as Knox went on, "Maybe I always have, but not till this instant, partner, did I know how badly."

KC shook his head, he couldn't quite figure out what Knox was saying no matter how hard he tried.

Knox chuckled grimly, "Don't think the irony is wasted on me, being a double negative myself, pal. I've been waiting for a real case of wrong to make Knox Chase all right. But who knew KC Green would get lost at the crime scene."

"I'm right here," KC exploded, "You're the one going somewhere."

"But you want to quit," Knox frowned.

If KC was being honest, all he wanted was to wake up from this nightmare and let some adult pick up the pieces, but he shouted "You're Wrong!"

Knox slipped further out of focus. "You think if it's a stacked deck anyway, why not fold. *I'm* just make-believe, *you're* delusional, and the truth must be whatever *they* say it is." The fading detective sounded more tinny and distant now. "Quit on me! Fine, I'm all wrong, anyway, it's part of my charm. But you quit on you... You quit on the case...?" Knox pounded his fist into his palm, "Then we're both crumbs on the counter, kid, that deserve to get swept away."

So much in KC's life weighed on him: his dad's case, his parents' marriage, Grist's vindictiveness, Ringmeyer getting hurt and Will in jail. Now this. The pain in his heart was plain for Knox to see, even as he continued dissolving on the spot.

"You gotta fight for what's right or our two wrongs make everything twice as wrong. Understand?" Knox demanded, and KC nodded, but he didn't have the faintest idea what Knox was talking about.

He just didn't want the detective to make the leap into nothingness, but his good friend kept dimming.

"Why do you think I took my lumps and never asked for sugar? Why do you think I let thugs with badges and heart-breakers without 'em work me over? Even when I was saying 'Farewell Cruel World' I never doubted that a happy ending was worth the price I'd pay. But you? You expect it'll just get written that way."

There was a knock on the door.

"KC, honey," his Mom tried, "Let's talk about this, bud?"

"But this is because of you and me. *We* did this," KC hissed on the verge of tears, but the detective just shook his head back at him, his signal modulating out faster and faster.

"That's not fair, KC," Mary pleaded from the hall. "Can I come in?"

KC whispered in a voice no louder than a breath, "I have to put an end to this."

Knox gritted his teeth, straining to hold on, "Will's not counting years on the clock because of me. And your dad didn't leave because of you. Hearing facts from a fiction smarts, sure, but you don't throw in the towel."

"You're leaving... throwing in the towel," KC cried.

"Am I?" Knox asked, almost completely faded from view.

KC gasped. This was it. Knox was going away, and he still didn't know why.

"I'm not going anywhere, KC," Mary demanded. "Let me in!"

"The only partner any man really needs is a mirror, just so long as you can look it in the eye," Knox said before trailing off inaudibly. Then he flared back into sight for a last word, "When you're in the dark, try it, and maybe you'll find... the truth's too close to see."

Then he was gone. Completely.

KC waited, not really believing it was possible, but Knox was nowhere now and out of his life. Another thing KC couldn't do anything about.

Mary opened the door and found him on the floor, in tears.

"I'm sorry, bud," she stooped over to hold him, but he broke away from her and scrambled to his feet.

"Get out of my room!" he shouted.

Mary Green didn't budge. "You don't get to talk to me like that."

KC didn't answer. He wiped away the tears as his whole body shook, glaring at his mom like he'd never forgive her.

"You know what I want more than anything, KC?" she asked without letting him answer. "To live here. Just the *three* of us. You, me *and your Dad*."

His breathing caught on the lump in his throat, but KC still didn't say a word.

"But I'll settle for living. Safe and sound and miserable as it may be, I want you and me to live. But instead, I think we're both waiting for your Dad to come back, and if something happened to you..., I'd never forgive myself."

She's worried. About me. KC decided. *That's why... This is my fault.*

"I did this?" he heaved sadly, and she shushed him.

"KC, it's not you."

"I'll make this right," he swore, wiping his nose and eyes, done crying anymore.

Suddenly he knew what he had to do. If he was hurting his Mom and Dad, or putting his friends in danger or getting Will into trouble, then KC had to take responsibility. *I can make it stop.*

She rushed over and hugged him to her quivering body, "KC, we both love you so much!"

His Mom ran her fingers through his hair and held him close, muttering "Growing up is....," but she just hugged him tighter, tapering off like whatever was in her head was too terrible to share.

He held her back. *It's not her fault.* It was him, and he could put an end to it. Tomorrow. Now they'd just huddle in the middle of his room, holding on to one another. KC wouldn't cry anymore because he knew what he had to do.

Chapter 24

Cat was whispering to Benjy in KC's chair when he walked into the classroom. He was ten minutes early but not early enough to beat his friends to school. They stopped talking as soon as he turned up and made hospital smiles in his direction. KC didn't have to be a world-class detective to deduce that their conversation was about him.

He marched over to break the news. He wasn't going to let Will take the fall for something bogus, and he didn't want his parents breaking up over him. Even if it wasn't a perfect solution or fair or right, he knew there was only one thing that he *could* do.

"Guys, there's--" he started to say, but Cat cut him off.

"Are you okay?" she asked.

"Yeah," he answered reflexively. "I'm doing, you know; but--" he really wanted to tell them what he'd decided.

"I'm really sorry about last night," Benjy broke in. "My mom, too, wanted me to wish you and your parents her best and let you know if there's anything she can do."

"Thanks," KC chuckled despite how miserable he felt. "But there's nothing she or anyone else can do. I shouldn't have gotten you and Will into this, and I'm getting everybody out of it."

Bridget Sosaurus sauntered inside wearing a long, clattering beaded necklace and a dreamy smile, and she asked loudly, "Mrs. Pepper! I couldn't find the janitor, and I need some supplies."

KC glanced at Mrs. Pepper who had obviously heard what happened to Will the night before because she responded somberly, "He... won't be in today."

"Oh," Bridget sounded concerned. Then her smile perked back up, and she looked over all the students before settling on Bobby G. "Well, Bobby, would you get me the special window cleaner Will uses and some rags from his closet?"

He lumbered out of his chair and rumbled to the door as Bridget smiled at Cat, KC and Benjy, explaining "I wanted the music room to sparkle today."

They nodded and turned back to one another to pick up where they'd left off.

"Okay, KC. What do we do now?" Cat asked.

"*We* don't do anything," KC got flustered. "*We've* done enough."

Cat and Benjy looked at one another.

"What?!" Benjy exploded.

"But Will is in jail, and he didn't do anything!" Cat insisted.

KC pulled a chair over. "I'm the one Grist has it in for. I'm going to confess to writing the note--"

Benjy cut him off, "You *didn't* write the note."

"I KNOW I DIDN'T WRITE THE NOTE," KC blurted out the obvious. He'd done a lot of thinking about this, and he knew what he had to do. "But Grist thinks I did. He wants to put me in juvenile hall, and if I give myself up he'll have to let Will go."

Benjy grimaced, but Cat pursed her lips and shook her head. "No. That's not right."

"It'll be fine. I'll get Will out, and maybe my parents won't have to--" KC went on, but Cat talked over him, even more certain than before.

"But KC, your note isn't what Will's in for."

"Okay, I'll tell him I wrote both notes," KC relented.

She cut him off in a tone that made everything sound so annoyingly obvious. "Will's in jail for running over Mr. Ringmeyer. I know he didn't do it, but no one will ever believe that *you* did. Think about it."

"Grist wants *me*," KC pleaded with her to stop debating.

"You're not thinking strategically," Cat warned, sounding a lot like Knox complaining that KC needed to be 29 steps ahead. "He's got Will, an ex-con, and all the evidence points to him. Even if you confess, which knowing Grist he'd let you do, he'd still nail Will. He'd get both of you."

KC shook his head. What she was saying was so true it hurt his brain to think about it.

Benjy turned to him and insisted, "We have to prove Will didn't do it, KC. It's the only way."

Like that's even possible?!

"And how do we do that? Hunh?" he huffed at Cat and Benjy, ticked at both of them for messing this up. "We can't. This is a great big set-up, and we're a bunch of dumb kids."

Cat took KC's hand in hers and looked him in the eye and said simply, "You're KC Green. You can do anything."

Her touch was electric and ran in a current down his back through his butt and into the seat of his chair, paralyzing him. KC couldn't move, except for the breath pumping in and out of his chest mechanically.

"We have to help Will," Benjy said, but KC couldn't stop looking at Cat who smiled encouragingly at him.

KC would have smiled back, except Bobby G came running into the classroom holding a hunk of metal and plastic wired together. Everyone gasped.

"I found this in Will's closet," Bobby shouted.

It looked like a time bomb made out of broom-sticks and duct tape and an egg timer, and it was thankfully not ticking.

Mrs. Pepper stood up and announced in a high-pitched falsetto that could have cracked glass, "Fire drill, class. Hurry!"

She leapt her way to the fire alarm again, and as soon as the claxon sounded, everyone got up and headed to the door except Cat, and KC and Benjy. They just looked at one another, Cat and KC still holding hands.

"For Will," he said, and Benjy put his hand on top of theirs and the three of them repeated his name.

"For Will."

Then they stood up calmly amid the chaos and walked out of the room.

Chapter 25

The kids had to wait outside while the police searched the school and examined what Bobby G had found. Cornelia cruisers ringed the playground, and county and state officers screeched to the scene. It was a circus with yellow caution tape and flashing lights, and after an hour it felt like the students were about to be dismissed and sent home. Pretty much everyone's parents had come to school to check on them, and a few kids had left already, but the teachers huddled together and agreed that it would be good to get back to normal. So all the kids who'd stayed were herded inside.

Evidently, the bomb was a fake, but Grist wasn't disappointed. He was gloating over all the good imprints he'd pulled for the fingerprint lab that he could match to his suspect. Bridget Sosaurus gaped with wonder at his every word, and KC knew it didn't look good for Will.

Back inside, he excused himself and headed straight for the bathroom, which he figured was the only place he could be alone. He didn't see anyone else and ran into one of the stalls where he unrolled a lot of toilet paper to plop on the seat before sitting down with his pants still on. He shut the door. Everything felt charged with energy.

"Okay," he whispered. "Knox, I need you."

He waited. KC hoped his former partner would show up on command, despite what happened the night before, but he didn't hear anything. Just the creaks of an old building in winter, he figured.

KC couldn't believe Knox wouldn't come back. He leaned up off the seat and opened the metal door and looked outside but didn't see anyone.

"C'mon," he practically shouted. "Knox, I really need you. What do you want me to say?"

He locked the door again and sat back on the seat.

"I'm sorry for saying it was your fault. At the pig farm, you told me not to tell the police what I knew." He waited for some answer, but there was just more creaky silence so KC chuckled.

"Right about now you'd usually say something incomprehensible like I didn't know what I thought I knew until I really knew it. I know that now, and I'm sorry I blamed you."

KC took a deep breath.

"I don't know what a double negative is, but I know you care about people besides yourself. You used to care about me, and I care about Will and doing what's right. And I really need your help, Knox..."

KC thought he heard something rustle on the other side of the door, and he ripped it open but only found

Benjy standing there looking at him, open-mouthed and astonished. "You were gone a while," he stammered.

KC didn't look away, though the light went out of his eyes when he realized Knox hadn't returned.

"I wanted you to know that we were going to chorus now," Benjy continued.

"Okay."

"I thought you weren't going to talk to him anymore," Benjy whispered, hurt. "It's not good to be talking to people who aren't there. I'm just worried about you, man."

"Well, don't be," KC brushed past him, out of the stall, "Because now Knox Chase isn't talking to me."

KC roared out the door, leaving Benjy just standing there.

≈≈≈≈≈≈≈≈≈≈≈≈≈

A gentleman would have given the German fair warning, but Knox Chase didn't know anyone fitting that description. Besides, the Übermensch leading 'Dorothy' at the end of his gun probably wasn't done reading Robert's Rules of Conduct, either.

Knox reached into his pocket for the sharp piece of slate he'd used to break into the building. One

edge fitted roughly like a handle
in his palm letting him grasp it
like a black-jack.

Knox light-footed out from behind
the door as the former waffen-SS
man stepped past. He swung hard,
leveling the stone like it was a
sledge hammer at a county fair and
brought it to bear wanting nothing
more than to ring this man's bell.

The layered slate sunk into the
former soldier's curtained locks an
inch above the cowlick. Then the
rock split in half. Blood flowed
in the feathery waves of the
German's hair, but instead of
passing out, he swung his gun
blindly at the detective.

Catching Knox with the barrel of
his Mauser across his left temple,
comets flared in the detective's
corneas, but he didn't stagger
back. He willed himself closer to
the man he'd attacked. The German
was an inch or two taller, but he
was too interested in killing and
couldn't level his gun with Knox on
top of him. Off-balance, he fired
the Mauser, and the bullet rocketed

past Knox's ear before ricocheting
in bursts down the cinder block
hall. Not that Knox could hear
anything besides the ringing in his
head.

The next shot wouldn't miss. So
Knox heaved from the shoulder,
steam-rolling his fist into the
German's belly with everything he
could bear. With the sharp-edged
slate still in it, the punch
landed, and the Kraut bent over,
gasping. Then Knox rocked the
soldier's head back like it was
driven on a piston with an upper
cut into his chin.

Welcome to New York, Knox thought,
watching the gun sail out of the
German's hand when his skull
smacked the wall behind him. The
man's eyes closed, and he slunk to
the floor, folding against the
linoleum like so much wet laundry.

Watching himself not get the gun after it flew out of the
German's hand made Knox want to shout at himself,
Never turn your back on a killer, no matter how pretty she is!

Knox searched the man's pockets and
found nothing incriminating. He

fished out his wallet, and his ID said his name was Sven Amundsen from Sweden, but the detective could get a license saying he was Warren Harding if he wanted one.

Then he located a photo of the German in civilian clothing in front of an old castle with some of his friends. Bratislavsky hrad, the inscription on the back read, 1942, and suddenly Knox knew that this man had served near Thereisenstadt during World War II.

A drop of Knox's blood dripped onto the German's wallet. He'd cut his hand on the slate, and the gash was deep and running. The red liquid pooled like mercury in a thermometer until it spattered on the man he'd knocked out.

The gong in Knox's head hadn't stopped ringing from the German's gun. He still couldn't hear out of his right ear, but he saw the shadow that crossed on top of him. Knox turned and saw Dorothy swinging the pistol butt right at his sore temple.

Knox worried. It's curtains for KC if I can't get out of this.

> **No time to duck or block, he watched as the beautiful woman knocked him unconscious with hardly a shrug. _You're welcome_ was the last thing he thought before everything went dark.**

≈≈≈≈≈≈≈≈≈≈≈≈

Back in chorus class, KC didn't have to say anything about not mentioning Knox. Benjy could tell the subject was off-limits. Besides, there were other things on his mind as they sat on the risers.

All the kids in the class, besides Benjy, chatted with their friends, excited about not having to learn or work. They couldn't have been happier, but he was watching Bridget Sosaurus and Charlie Grist giggle by the piano. He leaned forward trying to listen in on the two of them whispering, which was useless since they scrunched so close together. Every few seconds, though, they'd erupt laughing, and Benjy huffed in his seat as his face got redder and redder.

Their substitute and Bobby G's dad looked like school kids in love. It was totally weird. Grist was supposed to be investigating but didn't seem interested in getting to the bottom of anything other than how to woo Ms. Sosaurus. That didn't look like too much of a mystery, either, from the way she was clinging to every word he said.

Benjy brooded, eyes narrowed, staring at Grist and Bridget while Cat and KC tried to solve the mystery beside him.

"...But unless we can figure out what they're trying to steal, what and where this 'piggy' is, what are we going to do?" KC wondered.

Cat nodded, "I know."

Benjy wasn't listening, though. He fixated on Grist and Ms. Bridget who were off on a new round of giggles, and when she put her hand on his bicep, and he smiled and looked deep in her eyes, it was too much.

"That's it--" Benjy stood up.

He wound his way through the web of conversations across the bleachers, down to the piano. "Hem HEM," he cleared his throat by the detective's side.

Grist and Bridget grinned guiltily as she turned to Benjy. "Yes, honey?"

"Shouldn't we be rehearsing now?" Benjy insisted. "As a class," he glared at Grist. "Alone." He laid extra emphasis on the word in case the detective wasn't getting the message.

The two adults snickered. If they'd been drinking milk it would have sprayed out of their nostrils, all over Benjy.

Grist straightened up and smoothed out his suit. "I can take a hint," he started to go, but Bridget grabbed him.

"No," she barked.

Her voice sounded like she was training her dog not to pee on the carpet. Then she turned to Benjy and told him, "Ben, would you pass out the music sheets and bring me my book? Detective Grist is my guest."

Benjy frowned. He sulked for a second, and then he nodded, resigned to the fact that she seemed to like Grist, even if it made no sense to him. She whispered something that made the Cornelia detective go bright red before cracking up, and Benjy slinked away to the music rack.

He picked up the whole pile of materials to glumly wander through the stands handing out song sheets. As he approached Bobby G and his cronies, the bully was recounting what had happened that morning for the thousandth time.

"I mean, I didn't know the bomb was a fake. I thought I was saving everyone!" he clucked proudly.

Bobby's friends weren't bothered by the fact that he had brought the bomb *to* their classroom full of students instead of carrying it away. They just nodded in awe, but Benjy scoffed.

"You want to hear something--," Bobby pulled out his cell-phone, but when he saw Benjy sneering at him he cut himself off. "What's the matter, Benjy, jealous of my dad?"

Bobby and his buddies thought this was hilarious, and they fell all over themselves laughing. Benjy probably *was* jealous of Bobby's dad but didn't want to admit it. He took three music hand-outs and flung them at the gang before walking on to the next kids.

Instantly furious, Bobby shot his foot out, stopping Benjy's green sneakers cold. They ran headlong into an oversized pair of red high-tops, and their owner flopped to the ground, scattering papers everywhere with a strangled cry. Everyone went quiet.

Splayed on the ground, Benjy shook his head, disgusted, as Bobby laughed, "Have a nice trip? See you next fall!"

Grist chuckled, and Bridget scolded Bobby, "It's not nice to mock clumsy children."

Benjy groaned.

"You okay?" KC mouthed from atop the bleachers.

Benjy nodded and picked himself up and brushed himself clean. All the conversations roared back, and he gathered up the hand-outs and papers from all over the floor. An upside down brochure for the Amazing Asia exhibit slid the furthest.

Benjy flipped it over so it was facing front like everything else, and the 'Pagoda Pig' glistened on the cover. It was a foot-long treasure from the Tsing

Dynasty made entirely of giant rubies and emeralds and other massive gems. Tiny diamonds glistened in every joint, and the whole thing was sculpted from 24 karat gold.

It was glorious and invaluable. It was definitely IT. Benjy found the piggy, and he couldn't speak as his hands trembled.

He ran up the bleachers where KC was saying, "We know it's not a real pig, and it's--," but Cat saw the insane smile on Benjy's face.

"What?" she asked.

"Guys, I've got it," he spun the cover around to show them both.

They gaped at it.

Cat laughed, patting Benjy on the back, "You're a genius!"

KC took the museum brochure and stared, shaking his head and muttering, "The truth really is too close to see."

"What?" Cat asked.

Benjy grinned at him suspiciously.

"Nothing," KC chuckled. "Something somebody told me once."

Chapter 26

After school, Cat, KC and Benjy raced for their bikes. They would not stop for anyone, or pass go or collect $200. They had a lead that needed checking out, and they were bound and determined to check it. Besides, the day had already been so disrupted that none of the teachers tried to keep them and teach them anything, anyway.

They pedaled through the weirdly warm streets of Cornelia, their winter coats flapping open as they rode. Tons of people were strolling in the afternoon sun, but nobody minded the sight of three kids in a hurry to get somewhere as they sped along the sidewalk.

At the other end of Main Street, the Art Museum loomed. Its columns and archways and high ceilings probably made the mansion feel like a museum back when people were still living in it. The kids pedaled through the wrought iron gates and hopped off their bikes without stopping, running with the handlebars before ditching their rides in the grass.

There was a notice on the door in a plastic case, but they were in such a hurry that Benjy ran up the steps and shook the knocker three times before he stopped to read it. "Come back for tomorrow's Exciting Grand Opening! Amazing Asia, Treasures of the East. Doors Open at 8 am."

"Why do you think they call it 'The East'?" he asked. "My great-great-grandparents sailed east to get here. We should call it the West."

"But 800 years ago Marco Polo went east when he went to China, and so everybody still thinks of it as the East," KC shrugged.

"Well, I'm gonna call it *the* West," Benjy insisted.

"Cool." That made sense to KC.

"Guys," Cat interrupted. "There's got to be a back entrance where they take the art inside."

"Let's go to *the* back," Benjy said, and they all ran around the building.

The old kitchen had been converted into an oversized freight zone with a massive lift gate for 18-wheelers. Beside it, there were stairs leading to a heavy, white door with no label or sign on it. The kids tried it, and it was unlocked so they pulled it open to find themselves in the guts of the museum.

Distant hammering and heavy things rumbling echoed through the space. A long hallway stretched to their left, and they followed it, curving around a corner and winding up in front of a desk with a bulletin board mounted next to it. As they approached, though, Oona Pesce shouted from behind them, and they froze.

"What do you kids think you're doing here!" She marched over, her high heels tattooing the marble floor.

Ms. Pesce's nose was back to the same color as the rest of her skin, but her expression hadn't improved.

She growled, "Get out of here before I call the police."

"We want to see someone in charge," Cat stood her ground.

"I am in charge, and--" Oona Pesce started to say, but Cat cut her off.

"Excuse me. You said decisions were the responsibility of the exhibiting museum, so I'd like to speak with someone from *our* museum. Please."

An older Hispanic woman stepped in at the administration desk behind them, laughing, "The exhibit opens tomorrow, kids. Come back then."

She looked kind but frazzled, and KC promised, "We're going to," as the three kids approached the desk anyway.

"We're part of the concert," Cat assured her.

"Then you're early, and we're all too busy right now, gang," the woman replied.

"We need to see the pig." Benjy pulled the brochure out and pointed to the cover. "This pig. We need to see it."

"Do I have to call security, kids?" she sighed.

"About time," Oona Pesce grumbled.

"Yes," Benjy warned her. "We think someone's going to steal this pig, ma'am. Can you tell us when it got to the museum?"

The lady glared at them.

"We think someone's going to try and rob your museum, Mrs..." Cat waited.

"Mrs. Muebles," the museum woman frowned, her lashes forming a V. "I'm the deputy curator."

"Show her the sketch," Cat nudged KC.

"Oh, yeah," he pulled out the folded-up drawing he'd made for Grist.

Mrs. Muebles looked at it, and her frown grew into an O of astonishment as she gasped, "On Valentine's Day..."

She glanced up from the drawing to the kids, remembering, "It was chaos. The exhibition was arriving, and we were short-staffed - the one time I could have used a hand," Mrs. Muebles smirked at Oona Pesce, then she turned back to Benjy, Cat and KC. "He just stepped forward and gave me an envelope without saying a word. Since shippers and delivery men kept coming and going I didn't think too much of it, but he was... scary."

The kids nodded at her, and she continued, "Well, I opened it up and inside was just a cute Valentine's Card.

From some private investigator." Mrs. Muebles found the letter beneath her desk and held it out.

KC realized too late that this was *his* Valentine and reached out to grab the manila envelope, but Cat was standing closer, and since he couldn't just elbow her out of the way, she grabbed it and slid it open to devour the poem inside. KC couldn't breathe, and he couldn't rip his eyes from Cat's face as she read the card. He'd barely been prepared for this a few days ago, and so much had happened in the meanwhile. *Now, she has to get it?!* When his guard was down?!

Her eyes raced across each line and down the entire poem until she reached the finale and read those lines aloud to herself in a hushed whisper, "The gift I long to give, a heart-felt sign... Will you be my Valentine?"

Cat looked up at him with this gushy smile on her face, like her eyes were melting. She was getting red, and KC was sure that she was probably trying to find a way to let him down easy, since they were just friends now and working on a case. He looked away as fast as he could, and Mrs. Muebles giggled watching the two of them.

Benjy, however, was more interested in investigating, and he cleared his throat. "So then what happened?" he asked, which gave KC somewhere to look as he was studiously avoiding Cat's gaze.

Mrs. Muebles relived the moment, "Well, I laughed. I was relieved I suppose. It was just a love poem."

She grinned at KC, and he blushed. Now he couldn't look at Cat *or* Mrs. Muebles. His eyes roved over the room for somewhere safe to settle, and they landed on something peculiar on the bulletin board on the wall beside the desk.

"I gave it back to him," she went on. "I told him I was already married."

As embarrassed as KC was about the card, he studied the cork surface. It was meticulously arranged with non-overlapping flyers and spare, red push-pins in the bottom corner, except there were four thumbtacks not holding anything up. In between was a letter-sized gap where a flyer must have been and even a tiny, torn corner of whatever had been there before.

KC turned back to Mrs. Muebles, "He didn't think it was funny, though, did he?"

She shook her head and said, "He took it and looked at it and then slammed his hand on the desk and stormed out." Mrs. Muebles shrank away from the table, recalling how angry the stranger had been.

"Did you flinch and look away when he hit the table?" KC asked.

She nodded, eyes wide in surprise at how he could possibly have known this. Cat and Benjy gawked at him like he was a fortune-teller gazing into a crystal ball.

"One last question, Ma'am?" KC wondered in his best detective voice. "Do you know what flyer this used to be for?"

He reached up to the bulletin board and pulled down the scrap on the push-pin.

Mrs. Muebles took it from him and examined it closely but just shrugged, "No idea. Sorry," and KC took it back from her.

"Do you still want to see the pig?" she offered. "It didn't occur to me that was what he wanted. It sounds so stupid in retrospect, but it's one of the smallest pieces in the exhibit."

"The easier to make off with," KC noted. "No thank you, Mrs. Muebles."

Benjy and Cat looked at him confused, and he clarified, "We need to tell Will about this lead. Pronto."

"Anything you say, KC." Cat smiled then looked away nervously.

Benjy turned around to face Oona Pesce, "But there's something I want to know. Ms. Pesce, where were you when all of this happened?"

"That's none of your business," she glared.

"I thought it was a fair question, Oona. Where were you?" Mrs. Muebles chimed in.

"I told you. In that Grand View Hotel recovering from the riot the night before." She explained to KC, Cat and Benjy, "There was some police action in

Memorial Square at 1 AM on Valentine's Day! I couldn't get any sleep, and it set-off a bronchial inflammation. I spent all of the next day in bed. Sick. Case closed."

Benjy smiled. KC looked down when he realized she was talking about his investigation of Petunia up a tree that had made her sick.

"Are you accusing me of trying to steal something from my own exhibit?" Oona Pesce turned on Benjy.

"Well, what were you doing at our school again yesterday morning when we went to visit Mr. Ringmeyer?"

"This is ludicrous," Ms. Pesce fumed, but Mrs. Muebles glared at her until she hissed, "I was trying to get your principal to cancel this ridiculous concert."

Mrs. Muebles' lip quivered angrily. "Even though that's our decision?"

Oona Pesce sneered, "Some exhibitors need more help than others."

Then she brushed past the kids and stalked away.

Mrs. Muebles muttered something under her breath as she watched the exhibition assistant disappear around the corner, then she turned to the kids. "Thank you, children, for your help with this. I'll take it from here."

Chapter 27

The sun was still up, but it was casting longer shadows, and the kids shivered with their coats fluttering as they pedaled. Riding over to the police station, KC noticed that almost all of the hearts and red bunting that had adorned the town were gone. The pharmacy had clerks taping up four-leafed clovers and laughing leprechauns with fists drawn in the windows.

For KC, though, it was Valentine's Day all over. Maybe he hadn't blown it with Cat? After all, she hadn't told him that she didn't like him or thought his card was creepy. In fact, she kind of seemed like she liked it, and she kept smiling at him.

He got off his bike outside the police station, and Cat walked up to him, still smiling but her eyebrows knitted together, worried. "Just keep cool," she advised.

"What do you mean?" KC asked.

"We want to see Will, right?" she wagged a finger at KC kind of like a teacher would, "So we shouldn't call the detective a moron or anything."

"Even if he is a moron," Benjy contributed with a grin.

"Okay," KC agreed. "Thanks."

Cat flushed a little as she turned away from him, and KC thanked Knox in his head for the card he'd dictated just a few days ago. Then he thought back to Benjy's interrogation of the exhibition assistant.

"When you were talking to Ms. Pesce--" KC began.

"Rhymes with Mesh," Cat joked.

"Yeah, her. It sounded like you thought *she* was the one who was trying to steal the pig."

"Unh hunh," Benjy nodded. "You don't think she could have something to do with it?"

KC hadn't even considered the possibility, so he shrugged. "I guess not. I mean, she's a woman, and she's--"

"You have no idea what a woman's capable of," Cat chuckled.

"Think about it, she was conveniently MIA when the Pagoda Pig arrived at the museum," Benjy added. "And she doesn't want us to perform at the big opening. Maybe that's when she's planning to do the job! Plus, Mrs. Muebles hates her."

"Okay, I guess she *could* be involved," KC agreed, even though he couldn't see how.

The small police station officers' area wound around a corner with desks and cubicles, leading to two big offices behind. One belonged to Detective Grist. Since KC knew the way, and most of the officers and civilian assistants knew him, the kids were allowed to head back unaccompanied.

The policemen were talking to each other or managing calls with Cornelians concerned about bears messing up garbage cans or a little graffiti in an alley. One uniformed officer waved to KC, strapping on his gun-belt in mid yawn. Cornelia was the kind of town where when nothing happened it wasn't news.

The kids turned the corner for Grist's glass-walled office and were surprised to see Bridget Sosaurus sitting in the detective's lap behind his desk. They were holding hands, and both of them were watching something on his computer. It was cracking Grist up, but Ms. Bridget was cringing.

Then he looked up and glanced into the hall. Grist's face went red, and he pointed at KC before laughing so hard he couldn't breathe. Shaking, he pounded his desk, and Ms. Bridget stood up because his hysterics were knocking her off her perch. KC thought she muttered *poor, little guy* when he read her lips through the glass.

He froze, and Cat and Benjy looked at him. All three shrugged with no idea what was so hilarious.

Ms. Sosaurus wrinkled her face at them in sympathy and opened the door. "Hi, Gang," she invited them in with a sing-song voice.

KC nodded to thank her, but inside he was freaked out. Cat waved, and Benjy sighed before saying 'hi.'

KC felt like he'd been invited to dinner as the main course. Grist couldn't look at him without chortling and contorting, beet red.

"We're here to see Will Worth," KC announced as evenly as he could.

Bridget sat down on the edge of Grist's desk, and the detective got up and walked around beside her, still chuckling, "You are, are you?"

KC nodded, unsure what was going on.

"Charlie..." she warned Grist teasingly, draping a hand on his shoulder.

Benjy tensed up.

"Yes, sir." Cat piped in. "We'd like to speak with him."

"I like a good joke as much as the next guy," Grist giggled in KC's face, "but it's after visiting hours. You're too young to be in reception unsupervised, and you three are this close to being charged as--," but whatever he was about to arrest them for was lost as he squealed reflexively and scrunched his head into his shoulders.

Ms. Bridget was dancing her fingers up and down his neck. "Charlie," she scolded him. "You be nice to these kids. They're my students, and you know it's not easy for them."

She gestured at KC. All of this laughter and commiserating was starting to drive him crazy, but he kept his mouth shut because it looked like Grist might actually give in.

"...I don't know," the detective moaned, almost in physical pain at the prospect of being kind to the kids.

He shook his head at them before turning back to face Ms. Bridget, and with his attention elsewhere, KC and Cat dared to share an open-mouthed look of astonishment. Benjy kept his hands on his hips, though, glowering at Grist like nothing between them would ever be okay after stealing his woman.

"Would it hurt anything if these kids got to talk to their friend...?" Ms. Bridget cooed.

Grist thought it over as her fingers teased his chest through the buttons of his dress shirt.

Then her digits crept to his sides and tickled him, "Hummpph? Can't we share a little of our joy...? Please..."

He wriggled helplessly, unable to escape her grip.

Twisting and shivering and smiling despite himself, he turned back to the kids and giggled, "I guess..."

KC and Cat erupted in grins. She even clapped out of surprise, but Benjy was angrier than he had been. If you'd cracked an egg on his forehead just then it would have fried AND scrambled, he was that mad.

"There you go," Ms. Bridget released Charlie Grist and spread her arms wide. "Talk with your friend and tell him our big news. We--," but Benjy couldn't take it any more.

"We've got news, too," he interrupted. "We know what the thief is trying to steal."

"You do?" Bridget asked wide-eyed in her most encouraging voice.

Benjy nodded, pulling out the brochure from the museum, "This priceless pig in the Amazing Asia exhibit."

She took the brochure from him, her eyes glued to the pig on the cover.

"This person tried to get it on Valentine's Day when it arrived," Benjy went on, "but for some reason when the note got mixed up they didn't go through with it. And I think I know who it is..."

Bridget smiled at him, speechless, but Grist glowered down at all three kids. "So it's jewelry now that this pig pincher's after?" he asked Benjy who backed away a fraction of a step. Then Grist turned on KC, "Not livestock anymore? Or bank money?"

KC raised an eyebrow.

"Yeah, I know about that," the detective went on. "The Manager's been on my case since you visited him."

KC flashed-back to what Cat said.

They wanted to see Will not call Grist names or get thrown out of the station, so he took a deep breath and in the most respectful voice he could muster he said, "If you'd just ask Mrs. Muebles at the museum, she'd--," but Charlie Grist poked KC in the chest.

"It's a figment of your overactive imagination," he insisted, making KC swallow the rest of his words. "And if you kids don't drop this, I will arrest you. If not now..., when you-know-who steps down."

Grist gestured at Chief Williamson's office and didn't finish his sentence. None of them said a word, but KC died a little on the inside. It didn't matter if nothing ever happened in Cornelia. With a dingus like Grist in charge, the town didn't stand a chance.

"You got me?!" Grist nudged KC again, making him stumble backwards.

Cat's every muscle flexed, like she would have brained the detective with a saxophone if only she'd been holding one. Benjy moped at Ms. Bridget, longing for her to apologize and get back in his good graces. Meanwhile, KC stared at Grist as blank-faced as he could make himself while trying to figure out exactly what about this man could appeal to Ms. Sosaurus.

Grist must have had a similar concern, because he straightened himself back up and did his best imitation of a human being. "Now go see your friend, Will. And please tell him to come clean before things get any messier for him."

Benjy couldn't help himself and leaned over to whisper to Ms. Bridget, "You don't have to do this."

She looked at him. All the blood drained from her face.

Benjy gestured at Grist, "He's not the only one who thinks you're... amazing."

Ms. Sosaurus sighed, and her cheeks went pink again. "I can't tell you how lucky I am to find someone like Charlie."

Then she pulled him tight and snuggled him with all her might. Grist, however, never stopped glaring at the kids as they escaped on tiptoe, while their substitute teacher kept hugging him.

≈≈≈≈≈≈≈≈≈≈≈≈

The buzzer that admitted the kids into the downstairs reception area was loud and long, and it shook the teeth in their gums. The holding cells had been built about a hundred years before in the basement of the police station in the middle of a tunnel connecting the jail to the courthouse. Cages shielded fluorescent lights overhead, and bright turquoise paint clung to the cinder blocks, but otherwise the cold, damp place could have been a castle dungeon.

The three kids were led to a narrow bench just wide enough for their bottoms to fit if they scooched close together. Ahead of them was a 2 inch thick piece of plexiglass encased in a wire mesh on both sides.

Somebody had drilled one-quarter inch holes through the window meant for talking to the prisoner.

Another guard led Will to his chair opposite them and helped him into his seat since his hands were still cuffed behind him. Will smiled at the kids. It wasn't a big enough grin to reach his eyes, but he took a big, grateful breath of relief when he was alone with them.

"How are you?" Benjy asked.

Will's smile faded a little, "Well..." he considered his answer, "I'm hanging in there. But how about you? Any trouble with Grist?"

The kids' looked meaningfully at one another, and it was up to KC to say, "Not really," since he was the most convincing fibber.

"Yeah, right," Will smirked. "You need to stay out of trouble. Grist means business."

"Forget Grist," Benjy chimed in.

"We're working to get you out of here," Cat said.

Will shook his head. "I'm just going to get this over with." The kids looked at one another as he went on, "Grist says he can make things go easier for me if I confess, and it's not like I've lived a perfect life."

"No!" Benjy screamed, and the guard stepped forward to make sure they were all-right, only backing up when all three kids nodded that they were fine.

All three of them were afraid for Will, but even deeper, they were scared because this thing was so obviously unfair. *What if the truth doesn't matter?* No one in charge seemed to care. KC swallowed back a bitter taste rising in his throat. His blood pumped faster.

Determination tingled in his finger tips and in little sparks down his arms and across his back as he leaned forward and asked, "Did you do it?"

"No," Will mumbled, "but..."

"You didn't steal a car?" KC cut him off.

Will shook his head, trying to speak, but KC talked over him "Or attempt to kill Mr. Ringmeyer? Or build a fake bomb?"

"You know I didn't," he pleaded, "But I don't want you getting into any trouble."

KC smiled, "We'd rather get in trouble then see you confess to something you didn't do." He turned to Cat and Benjy, "Right?"

They nodded.

"There's nothing anyone can do," Will's voice rasped.

Benjy perked up and pulled out the museum brochure to show Will. "Look, we figured out what the piggy is, and where it is.",

Will stared at The Pagoda Pig, dumbstruck that he was sitting in a cell for something so... small.

"We're going there tomorrow for the concert," Cat said, studying Will's eyes as they pieced together how this could be possible from a picture on a brochure. "Don't do anything until you talk to us, okay?"

Will looked up from the pig and moaned, "My finger-prints are on a bomb... What are you guys gonna do? What else can I do? I need this to end."

KC took the brochure from Benjy and pointed to the statue. "Would you kill Mr. Ringmeyer to get this?"

"Of course not," Will gulped in horror.

"Well, somebody out there tried to, and they'll do it again, and if you give in, you're helping them."

Will frowned as KC went on, "I'm not going to let them get away with this, hurting people for a thing they'll melt down for so many dollars a pound, but you have to believe in yourself if you want anyone else to. Understand? And if that means that we take some knocks, well... happy endings don't write themselves."

Something flickered to life over KC's shoulder, but none of the others could see it, and he was concentrating all of his energy on Will so he didn't notice.

A deputy walked over and put a hand on the prisoner's shoulder. "Time's up, Worth."

"What do you say?" KC asked.

Cat was watching him, riveted, but she turned to Will as he stood up.

"I've got to go. Thanks for coming, guys..." he said.

"Will..." Cat called after him.

He smiled back at them over his shoulder as the Deputy steered him away by his cuffs.

Chapter 28

RIDING HOME...

The kids didn't talk much, biking home after sunset. Riding alongside one another past quiet houses in the darkness, mercury vapor lamps lined their route, making bright circles in the pavement. KC hadn't been able to shake a bad feeling since they left the police station, like somebody was watching him, but he didn't know who.

He adjusted the rear view mirror on his bike and swerved when he caught sight of Knox Chase beaming at him over his left shoulder.

"Whoa!" KC almost rode into Cat before he steadied his eighteen-speed. "Where did...?"

Cat laughed, "I've been here the whole time, KC...,"

Knox chimed in, "I only caught the end of your talk with Will, so I can't say if he was listening, but *she* got an earful. And would gladly ask for seconds if you know what I mean."

KC blushed and looked over at Benjy who was staring at him suspiciously.

Knox got the hint, "Yeah, we don't need to give the whole show away, but I want you to know something. You bought me a second chance, Partner. Whatever you been doing, keep doing it, because you can't put a price on living."

"So, everybody's okay?" KC asked as generally as possible.

"Actually, I feel terrible," Benjy answered. "I mean, I can't imagine being accused of something you didn't do with no way to prove you were innocent."

Knox remarked, "That guy's got real potential..."

"We have to help Will," Cat insisted.

"Ummh..." KC agreed.

He was so grateful to have Knox there that he kept cheating his gaze to the mirror to listen to him, not wanting to lose him again.

"Everything was dark," Knox recounted. "My cheek glued to the mat, it was past nine on the ten-count, and I was listening for 'you're out.' No idea if I'd see you again, I'll tell you one thing--"

He was about to go on, but KC caught a glimpse of a large bakery truck racing towards them with its headlights turned off. It appeared in the pool of a street-lamp and then disappeared back into shadow. In the glimpse he stole through his semi-transparent friend, KC could have sworn the stranger was behind the wheel.

"Disappear!" KC shouted so Knox wouldn't block his view, and then he hollered to his friends, "Dump the bikes! Get off the road!"

Cat and Benjy looked at him confused and froze, but Knox saw the vehicle bearing down on them and flickered away. The driver gunned the engine. Twenty-five feet, fifteen feet separated them from the steel bumper. Almost too late, Cat and Benjy looked up.

"Jump!"

KC leaped off his 18-speed onto Cat and toppled with her to the grass beside the road.

Five feet from the truck, Benjy laid his bike down and ran to the other lawn just ahead of the rig which swerved to get him. The delivery truck crushed their tires, smushed their frames and mangled their handle bars in a grinding, compacting symphony of destruction, but Benjy ran away to safety, and the vehicle rumbled off down the street.

The kids held their breath, waiting to see if the driver would back up and try hitting them again, but the bakery truck roared into the distance as house-lights on both sides of the street flicked on.

"Are you okay?" KC asked Cat who was beneath him in the grass.

She swallowed and nodded yes. "You saved my life," she gasped.

"No..." KC shook his head.

It was just luck that he'd been talking to Knox.

"Yeah, you did," Benjy got up and started crossing the street to interrogate him. "Why were you looking in your rear view mirror like that?"

"Just a... feeling I had." KC had been spooked since the police station, so it wasn't a total lie.

"Really lucky coincidence," Benjy said like he knew what KC had been doing.

"Not lucky enough to save our bikes, though," KC joked, getting up and nudging a frame with his toe. It was curved in the middle, perfect for riding in circles, but not for going anywhere ever again.

Cat laughed too loud and too long. In shock from their near miss, she giggled just grateful to be okay. Benjy, though, looked at his friend like the cat was out of the bag.

KC picked up what was left of his bicycle and wheeled it on the uncrushed rear tire. "We should get walking. If anybody calls the police, Grist is gonna write *us* up for littering."

Cat laughed again and grabbed her bike, which she could carry the short distance to where she lived. Benjy picked up what was left of his 10-speed, rolling it on the front tire awkwardly as they walked off for her house.

"What do you think?" Benjy asked.

Cat beamed at KC, "I think we're lucky to be alive."

"Sure," Benjy barely acknowledged, "But how'd they know to come after us? The only person we told about all of this was Grist... Do you think?"

Knox re-materialized as KC asked, "Do I think what?"

Benjy squirmed, "I mean, he'd almost have to be working for the burglars to be this stupid, wouldn't he?"

Cat shrugged her shoulders like it was eminently possible.

Benjy pinched his lip and went on, "I tell him somebody's trying to rob the museum, and he threatens to arrest *us*?! And then someone tries to run us over?"

They stopped at Cat's house. Everyone waited for KC's answer, but he took his time, not wanting to dismiss Benjy's notion without really considering it. Then he shook his head.

"It's suspicious, but he's really a lot dumber than you'd think. Plus, it wasn't Grist behind the wheel. It was the ransom note stranger."

Knox interjected, "Can you be sure?"

KC looked at him reflexively, "I'm sure."

He was a little out of practice hiding his invisible friend, but Cat shrugged it off and said, "I'll see you tomorrow, Benjy," and gave him a quick hug.

Then she ran to KC and squeezed him tight.

So tight, the breath in his chest coughed itself out, and she pulled him even closer, lifting his feet off the ground as she whispered, "Thanks..." with a soft warm breath in his ear.

Then she put him down and hurried up the steps to her door before he could say anything. Without looking back or waving, she opened it up and disappeared inside.

They stood looking at Cat's house for a second.

KC turned to his friend and asked, "Do you think she likes me?"

"Probably, man," Benjy steamed, "But there's more important stuff to deal with right now."

KC'd been feeling flush and pleased, especially considering that somebody'd just crushed his bike while trying to kill him.

"I'm sorry that I roped you into this," he said, but Benjy brushed that off, too.

"I'm your friend, and I'm not that afraid of getting killed or something, but you're scaring me right now."

KC snuck a look over at Knox, and Benjy pounced on it. "He's here right now, isn't he?" Benjy demanded.

KC sighed and walked away towards their houses, but Benjy pursued him. "He's back, right? And you're talking to him again, and that's why you were looking in the mirror?"

"Yes," KC groaned, "And that's why you're not dead by the way. So, you're welcome."

Benjy guffawed, "Well, don't forget to thank Mr. Chase for me, KC."

KC looked up at Knox who shrugged. "Tell him he's welcome."

"He says, 'You're welcome,'" KC repeated.

Benjy threw his hands up in the air huffing *Sheesh!* and walked off.

Then he stalked back to KC, his finger pointing in his face, "Friends don't let friends talk to make-believe friends, KC! I'll see you tomorrow...," and Benjy stormed off towards their houses, leaving KC and Knox standing on the sidewalk, watching him go.

"Sorry about that, compadre," Knox volunteered.

KC nodded at him and started walking slowly home. Knox trudged along beside him, quietly, both of them bogged down by heavy loads.

"You're not just a figment of my imagination, are you?" KC finally put his worry into words.

Knox shook his head.

"Though, of course, you wouldn't tell me if you were..." KC realized.

Knox admitted, "It's a pickle."

"Then tell me why you're here," KC insisted.

"I've had eleven years of thinking up the answer to that question, but I couldn't have told you until I came to in that jailhouse."

KC looked deep into Knox's weathered expression hoping to unriddle at least one puzzle.

"You know that despite living to a hundred, the old man who dreamed me up stopped writing me a long time ago? de Labios, my author?" Knox half asked and half told KC, who nodded.

"For the longest, I assumed he was sore with me. I mean, he made me everything I am, put me through the wringer and then left me in the rain all over again, but I thought maybe he felt like he'd fallen short," Knox confessed.

KC frowned at him, not understanding.

"My big fade began with the overgrown boys in tights and capes. These guys had super powers. I may have been made-up but they were make-believe. Even physics wasn't so powerful it could stop these phonies from doing what they pleased, and suddenly the world didn't care about fixing what was broken anymore," Knox expanded.

"What's this got to do with me?" KC asked.

"What's the score?" Knox smiled at him. The pulp fiction hero took a deep breath. "You and me. We can fix what's really broken. Right actual wrongs. We take on the chiselers, and the know-nothings, the corrupt and the care-nots. Then you put it down in black and white so people can't turn their heads away like it's okay."

"I'm supposed to do all that?" KC asked, too afraid to laugh. "Go around finding lost causes and fix 'em up?"

Knox nodded, "There's nothing like a lost cause for finding out who you ought to be."

KC stared at him in disbelief. Four days ago, he just wanted to talk to a girl he really liked. They were approaching his house.

"I'm calling my Dad," KC pulled out his cell-phone.

Knox joked, "What's he got that I don't?"

"Flesh and blood," KC dead-panned as he hit the speed dial.

"Clever... See, you've got what it takes," Knox smiled. "And you're welcome, by the way."

"For what?" KC asked while listening to the phone ring.

"For saving your life back there," Knox started fading away.

"I did that!" KC shouted back.

Knox shrugged with a grin, "Have it your own way!" Then he disappeared.

Ron Green answered the phone, "KC! Where are you and where have you been? Your mom called me, she's worried sick."

"Sorry, dad. I had to turn my phone off in jail."

Ron shouted "What?!" so loud that KC had to pull the speaker away.

"I know you told us not to keep investigating, but we've nearly got this thing solved. We found out what he's going to steal," KC informed him. "It's this emerald and ruby covered pig."

"A jewel covered sculpture?"

"Yeah," KC answered. "From the museum where we're giving the concert tomorrow, and we had to tell Will so he doesn't do anything stupid between now and when we catch the guy."

"Hang on, KC. Are you doing okay?" Ron asked, sounding strange.

KC had no single answer to that question. He was awesome: Cat not only liked him but maybe like-liked him. He was scared: somebody had just tried to kill him. He was thrilled: they missed.

"Yeah," KC summed it all up in a word. "Why?"

"Cause your mom told me that you're having a tough time."

"What do you mean, Dad?" The silence on the other end of the phone made him nervous.

His Dad spit it out, "Are you seeing things?"

All the blood in KC's body rushed to his face, and he felt like throwing up. There was only one honest way to answer that question, and Ron took his son's loss for words as a resounding Yes.

"Your mom said some kid has a tape of you talking to-- not yourself, really, but to Knox Chase? Is that possible, KC?"

Friends don't let friends talk to make-believe friends... Did Benjy record me? No Way. Un unh. *Then who could it be?*

KC remembered Bobby G in chorus class huddling around his phone with his friends, *and Grist laughed his butt off when he saw me.* He and Ms. Bridget were watching something on his computer. It had to be when he was in the bathroom after the bomb scare. *All those creaks..., and I wasn't paying attention.*

"It's possible, Dad," KC admitted. "Maybe Bobby G was lurking on a toilet and caught me asking Knox Chase for help with my case."

Ron sighed over the phone, "KC, it's all in your head, son, and all of this... we're gonna help you with. Help you see that this case isn't real."

KC cackled in disbelief, heaving from how *not* funny that was. He was wheeling his smashed-up bicycle to his front step after someone had just tried to kill him and cracking up about it. His emotional speedometer surged past sad and all the way around again... to hysterical.

Him laughing like this must have sounded like proof to his Dad that KC was going nuts, but the fact that Ron Green thought their biggest problem was KC's over-active imagination was too funny not to laugh.

"I'm not complaining about your help, Dad," KC's giggles were winding down. "And I'm not complaining about the fact that you can't help because you're working on your case. It's a really important case, and I don't blame you for picking your case over me. But if that's what you pick, then I've got this. Okay?"

Ron Green shouted, "There is no case, KC!"

KC swallowed another chuckle, "Okay, but my imaginary suspect just missed killing me and my friends tonight, and even if I'm too crazy to be trusted you can take their word for it."

"What are you talking about, Bud?!" Ron demanded.

"I've got to get back to dragging my smashed bicycle home after the imaginary stranger crushed it with a bakery truck, twenty minutes ago. So, I'm gonna go, but I'll be home in thirty seconds, and then we can all figure out just how insane I really am."

KC didn't wait for his father to answer before hanging up the phone and opening his front door.

He plopped his bike on the porch and walked in only to be greeted by his mother who shouted, "KC, are you hallucinating?!"

Chapter 29

INFAMOUS...

Mary Green looked paper thin, like this could tear her in half.

She knelt down in front of KC, trembling and teary and asked, "Are you talking to Knox Chase on the Case, bud?"

Bobby's video of him and Benjy had evidently gone viral, at least in the town of Cornelia, and Mary Green had watched the thing over a hundred times waiting for KC. When he finally showed up, she swore he'd get *the help he needed*. KC doubted it was the kind of help he was looking for, though, since she hollered at him when he told her that they'd almost been run over.

Cat knows was all he could think about as his mom lectured him. Bobby'd recorded everything from when KC shouted "C'mon" and walked back into the stall, through him telling Benjy that Knox Chase wasn't talking to him anymore. Then he put it online. *There's no way Cat will even talk to me anymore.*

If KC was watching somebody else do all of that stuff in a video, he'd know the kid was howling at the moon. *Case closed, I'm insane.* He couldn't laugh anymore, picturing himself locked in a tiny room in an uncomfortably snug white jacket for the rest of his life. His stomach was churning.

"How long has this been going on?" Mary trembled.

"Since Dad left," KC admitted. "That's when Knox showed up."

She smiled, and a tear rolled out of her eye, and she sniffled it back saying, "We're gonna get you help, bud."

That's what KC had been asking for since this stupid case started, and he shot to his feet, saying "Great!"

He walked to the front porch with his mom screaming, "Where do you think you're going?"

"To bring my bike in. Since it's evidence."

He dragged in what was left of his ninth birthday present. Mary Green looked at the bent frame and crushed tire. KC's bicycle was as thin as a tube of toothpaste where it had been smushed by the truck trying to kill him.

She gasped and went white. "What happened?!"

"I told you. A truck nearly ran over me and Cat and Benjy."

She may not have believed him before, but she wasn't going to let someone squash her son like a bug. Mary Green called the Cornelia Police, as did Cat's and Benjy's parents, and because Detective Grist had swapped shifts with a patrolwoman for personal reasons, a competent police officer came around to take their stories.

She had a pen, a notepad, a dozen intelligent questions and after taking all 3 kids' accounts independently and looking at their bikes, she put out an All Points Bulletin matching KC's drawing. She even asked him to make a copy so she could enter his picture into evidence.

After the policewoman left, it was so late his mother gave up questioning KC, but only because he was passing out in his chair. They argued over whether or not he'd be allowed to go to the concert the next morning, but since it was part of school and he hadn't actually done anything wrong, she relented and said yes.

"Don't worry, Bud," she told him. "We can tighten up your loose screws."

KC rolled his eyes, and she kissed him on the forehead. Then he went up to bed as she called his Dad. KC didn't want to speak to him again. He collapsed on the sheets without undressing or talking to Knox or thinking about how awful tomorrow would be.

≈≈≈≈≈≈≈≈≈

KC got up for school early, before his mom. She'd probably been awake all-night worrying about him and didn't hear him getting ready. He put on his trademark fedora hat and trench coat, strapped his pack across his back, grabbed a banana and walked out the door for the long, lonely walk to school.

In the Roosevelt Elementary driveway, a mini-bus idled. Smoke puffed out of the exhaust, and steam melted off the ice on the hood. The sun glinted off the glass into KC's eyes so he couldn't see how many people were on board already, but the door was open and he climbed inside.

When KC appeared on the stairs, one boy leaned to another and said "Oooooooh," like somebody had just gotten in trouble.

A handful of his classmates were sitting on the benches, and KC concluded they had all seen the video since it only took a millisecond for everyone to start whispering. He breathed deep and walked past snickers and stares to plant himself on an empty 3-seater in the middle of the bus. He was waiting for Benjy to show up to find out if *anyone* was willing to talk to him. KC figured Cat probably just pitied him now, but maybe, somehow, they could still be friends. If not, if he was too weird to be tolerated, he'd understand.

Lorrie snapped him out of his daze when she marched over, asking, "Are you okay?"

He looked her in the eye and couldn't decide whether or not she was being kind, so he just nodded warily.

"You're not going to hurt anyone today?"

She was patronizing him because he was *such* a violent lunatic. The kids around them cracked up.

"So far so good, Lorrie." KC worked hard not to let his voice crack. "Thanks."

"Well, keep it that way," Lorrie snapped then spun back around and returned to her seat as the kids on the bus hooted their approval.

KC breathed deeply and concentrated all of his attention on his fingers going white in his lap as he squeezed his two hands together. He struggled to remember why he'd insisted on coming to this concert.

All the while, new nicknames kept bursting in the air, 'Freak...' 'Nuts...' 'Looney...' Every time a new kid got on the bus, there were more sneers whispered just loud enough to see if KC would go nuts. If not for Will and Mr. Ringmeyer and his friends who'd nearly been killed trying to unravel this mystery, he'd have been much better off staying in bed. For the rest of his life.

"Knox, I really need you," Bobby G moaned in a high-pitched impersonation, and KC's head shot up. The bully's lips puckered in a put-on sad face. "I'm sorry for saying it was your fault. At the pig farm, you told me not to tell the police what I knew..."

Bobby's friends laughed along as he marauded down the aisle, but this time everyone else joined in, too. Hatred burned through KC as he stared him in the eye. His muscles ached.

Bobby G leaned closer to growl, "And if you ever mess with me again--," but KC never got to hear the rest of the threat.

Cat's cast whizzed through the air and thwonked Bobby on top of his head. Hard. So hard the plaster cracked a little beneath her wrist.

Tears formed in Bobby's eyes as he screamed, "Owh! What gives?"

He whirled and saw Cat standing there, blood red and fuming. "If you ever hurt my friend again, you will sing falsetto for the rest of your life. ¡¿Comprende?!"

"What's the matter, son?" Grist hollered from outside the bus.

A mean smile bloomed across Bobby's lips until Cat held up her cast. "And I'll tell your Daddy and everyone else who did *this* to me."

Bobby frowned, rubbing his head, but he muttered to his Dad, "Yeah, I'm okay."

"Now, get out of my way," Cat hissed at him.

Bobby turned around, fuming, and stalked to the back of the bus. Cat glared at him the whole way, then she sat down beside KC as kids started whispering all around.

"Are you okay?"

Unlike Lorrie, she really meant it, and KC swallowed before nodding, but the smile he was trying to fake never made it to his lips. She gazed at him until he raised his head and looked her in the eyes. Her expression promised that it would be okay.

"Do you really see this Knox Chase guy?" she whispered.

He sighed and chuckled, nodding. This time he managed to smile but only because of how miserable he felt.

"Is he here now?"

He shook his head.

"That's a shame, because we could really use his help," she smiled, and her smile reached her eyes, and he had to sniffle as she went on. "And when you see him, thank him for saving our lives last night."

She rubbed his arm with both of her hands, and it was like a firework burst in his heart. All at once, pins and needles tickled every nerve ending, and KC felt like summer despite the cold outside.

Cat didn't hate him. She didn't feel bad for him. Maybe she didn't like-like him, but who knew? Anything was suddenly possible.

He wiped his eyes and smiled, and then he looked at her cast with the crack in it. "Are you okay? Is your wrist all-right?"

She nodded that it was fine until she admitted, "It totally kills..."

Then they both cracked up, practically falling on top of each other. They giggled so hard everyone on the bus no-doubt thought KC was contagious, but neither of them cared. He wasn't sure why her aching wrist was so funny, but it was just good to be sitting next to her and maybe the feeling was mutual.

They kept laughing until a man who looked like a handsome, human version of Charlie Grist stepped aboard. He was wearing a tight Italian tailored jacket with matching pants, a silk tie and a crisp white shirt. Amazingly, his crumb-catcher moustache was clean-shaven away.

The transformation was so complete, the kids weren't even sure it was Grist until he leaned over the bench in front of them and snarled, "You kids couldn't even let me get married in peace?!"

The snarl was unmistakably his, and right behind him, Benjy was climbing the steps. He shook his head like his ears were malfunctioning and said the word *married* to himself like it had lost all meaning.

KC and Cat looked at one another, and the detective pursed his lips. "Old Chief Williamson delayed our honeymoon until today. All because of you and your cock and bull story about some 'stranger.'"

"Honeymoon?" Benjy repeated to Grist, like he'd been speaking another language.

All the color drained from his cheeks, and he wavered in the aisle like a willow quivering. Meanwhile, *Mrs.* Bridget *Grist* bounced up the stairs behind him in a white sundress, an open parka and a broad brimmed bonnet with a large backpack across her shoulders.

Her every tooth gleamed as she screamed, "Isn't it great! And my *husband's* driving us to the concert on the way to our Honeymoon!-- Pardon me, Ben."

Benjy stumbled past Grist in a daze and staggered onto the bench beside Cat. Mrs. Bridget leaned in and planted a big wet smooch on her husband's pucker that left him grinning.

"Honeymoon...?" Benjy wondered to himself, shaking his head over and over again.

Chapter 30

KC, Cat and Benjy didn't talk much while they waited for the short ride to begin. Once all the kids were aboard, Grist stalked back to the driver's seat and fussed with the bus controls. Still wearing her backpack, Mrs. Bridget clutched a massive purse and hauled an oversized canvas bag filled with poles to hold up the banners the kids had drawn.

She deposited the poster stands in the walkway and then clunked down the aisle to sit next to Bobby G in the back of the bus. She carefully took her pack off and snuggled up next to him, pulling out a diagram which she patiently explained. He smiled wide, but his complexion turned greener and greener the more that she said. He'd only known this woman since Tuesday, twice as long as his father had known her, and he looked like he was concentrating thickly on what she told him.

She spoke in a soothing, maternal tone, and he nodded along earnestly, but his brow kept furrowing deeper and deeper. KC almost felt bad for him, struggling to keep up with what she said and make a good impression, but when Benjy heard Mrs. Bridget cooing to her new stepson, his head whipped around jealously.

Eventually, he got over the shock and let his friends know that his mother had utterly freaked out about the whole smushed bike thing. KC was absolutely never allowed to come to his house again, but Benjy said he didn't care, and they'd still be best friends. He thought it might even be good for him to stand up to his mom. He smiled, but then the bus pulled away from Roosevelt Elementary, and he went back to brooding about Mrs. Grist.

In front of the museum, Bobby's buddies unloaded the canvas bag before anyone else was allowed to stand up. Bobby didn't actually help, but he held the plan that Mrs. Bridget had made for him, and he barked instructions to show her how serious he could be.

"Straight line... You kids, wait your turn... Hustle!" Bobby officiated from the curb as Grist gazed at him adoringly from the driver's seat.

KC and his friends were nearly the last ones off the bus, and he turned to them as they were approaching the museum. "Keep your eyes open."

Cat nodded as she walked past, but Benjy just shook his head sadly, still muttering "honeymoon..."

The foyer of the museum was a grand hall with dual staircases opposite the entryway. An arcaded passage led into the depths of the first floor in between them.

Originally built for cocktail balls and railroad receptions, this room had marble floors and scalloped wall sconces where stone statues in red, green, black and white loomed. The effect was cathedral-like, with high ceilings and thick leaded windows, but something in the middle of the room sparkled so brightly everything glistened.

The Pagoda Pig shined atop a glass covered plinth in the center of the room. Big city museums might try to lure patrons deeper into their collections by promising that the best was yet to come. Here in Cornelia, the curators just wanted to make sure the locals made it inside at all, so they positioned the biggest attraction by the front door.

High windows all around ignited the inset diamonds of the 16th century sculpture. The rubies and emeralds seemed to glow from within. As you approached the tiny creation, it was only sixteen inches long, the greens and reds and blinding whites sparkled and made you dizzy.

Cat, KC and Benjy walked in last but were immediately transfixed by the carnival reflections in the faces of their friends. Shimmering prisms shone in glints and rainbows, making the enormous room look like a jewel box for this one miraculous treasure. As other kids moved off to help Bobby and Mrs. Bridget put up the banners, they finally glimpsed the Pagoda Pig, and it made each of them gasp.

"It's beautiful," Cat stammered.

Not taking his eyes off the sculpture, Benjy nodded, only managing a "Wow..."

KC could have spent the rest of the day watching as the sun's slow progress captured different facets of each of the Pig's hundreds of gems, except a friend of his picked that moment to show up. "Glad you've found an appreciation for the finer things," Knox interrupted, "but don't you think you ought to case the place for trouble?"

KC nodded. He shook his skull to clear the sleepy dazzle out of his eyes. His head tingled, and his breath burned as he surveyed the mammoth hall. Echoes rebounded off the high ceilings, and everything seemed mystically important as KC strained to figure out if any of it mattered.

The room overflowed with laughing kids and barking adults. Girls giggled in the corner, a boy shoved his friend past a Greek statue, and KC saw Bridget rushing over to Bobby G in a barely contained fury, waving a paper in his face.

"I said the banners go here and here, not here and here." Her finger pounded the places on the diagram, and Bobby nodded along with every word as his mouth sagged open, and his eyes glazed from too many details.

A hazy lack of comprehension was written all over his face.

"Just get my sheet music, Hon," she dismissed him and commandeered his friends to position the posters exactly where she wanted them.

"Yeah, it's pretty," KC said with his back turned to the Pig as he wandered off, leaving Cat and Benjy unaware that he'd gone.

"Do you see anything?" Knox wondered.

KC didn't answer, checking the place with his eyes, ears and feet.

He watched Grist clapping his hands pointlessly, clamoring "C'mon, c'mon people, we need some organization here," with no one listening to him since he wasn't actually organizing.

KC ambled over to two boys conspiring in the corner. They looked shiftily back and forth before one of them passed the other a trading card. After a quick inspection and a satisfied nod, it disappeared and turned into a pack of gum.

Past them, Lorrie insisted into her cell-phone, "You never come to my performances, ugh," and she hung up. She glared at KC and marched away, and he knew she was just fighting with her parents.

He turned around, and behind him, Bridget maneuvered the last banner into position. "Now, that's more like it."

The posters on their high stands formed a towering trapezoid around the Pig's plinth. Something about them made KC look again. They faced in different directions instead of being turned towards the audience.

Mrs. Bridget evidently loved them, though, because she spun around, laughing, with the brim of her bonnet twirling over her face. *Must be excited about the concert*, KC thought. He kept his eye on her, though, as Bobby G shuffled over with her things.

Mrs. Bridget's new step-son huffed and hustled with his head down as she kept twisting. He hurried until his sneaker squeaked on the marble floor, and he tripped, slamming into her out-stretched right hand with a book that snapped four of her fingernails off.

"Oh, man..." Bobby gasped, shaking his head.

KC didn't look at Bobby G, though. He walked closer, transfixed by Bridget's hand *without* its long red nails. She shook it briskly, smiling at Bobby.

"Don't worry, sweetie. They're fake," she reassured him and held out her fingers for him to see that there was no damage done.

KC suddenly remembered hands in the exact same position. On Valentine's Day outside the Antique Boutique, those very digits had taken his card for Cat by mistake. At least he thought they were the same.

"KC?" Knox asked like he knew what made his friend's jaw drop and his eyes go wide.

KC didn't answer. He walked around to get a better view of Mrs. Bridget's face. He had to be positive. In his mind, he saw the Stranger's delicate neck-line concealed by a stubbly beard and high collar.

Bridget's jaw was exactly the same but clear and smooth now without make-up for impersonating Will Worth.

"Fake," KC muttered, a rush of understanding tattooed across his expression, and from halfway across the hall Bridget saw him, and all the color drained out of her cheeks.

He knew, and she knew he knew as he spun around to look for help.

Chapter 31

"Bridget's the stranger," KC muttered.

Knox nodded and counseled, "Time for the cops to earn their pay."

KC looked for help, but he couldn't see a security guard in the crowd of kids and chaperones.

He spun a little more and saw Grist with his back to the action, pinning two kids against the wall, shouting "Littering?! In the museum?!"

KC pivoted again, this time looking for his friends. He found Cat with Mrs. Bridget grasping her by the shoulder. Cat wasn't resisting, and her eyes apologized.

Bridget pulled out a small, black metallic object she'd been pressing against two of Cat's ribs. No one else noticed across the crowded room, and she tucked it back out of sight and smiled so innocently that all of her beautiful teeth gleamed. Then she jerked her head, signaling KC to walk towards her.

While he had been looking for reinforcements, their music substitute had taken the girl he liked hostage. It was obscene. She masqueraded as someone totally nice, but KC could see she'd do whatever it took to get what she wanted. So, he did what she wanted. He raised his hands slightly before him so she wouldn't hurt Cat, and he walked slowly over to her.

Knox was beside him, baring his teeth, "Keep her talking so the rod won't have to."

KC nodded then promised Cat, "I'll get you out of this."

Bridget smiled and cooed to him in sugary sweet tones while pressing her weapon against Cat's back-side, "No funny business."

She sounded completely insane and Knox mused, "The head shrinkers would have a field-day with her."

KC agreed.

Meanwhile, Benjy had missed the whole thing. Having wandered around to the other side of the Pig, he was still so dazzled that he hadn't noticed what was happening, which was lucky. KC figured he'd raise the alarm when he saw they'd disappeared.

Bridget hissed through a sharp grin, "Down that hall, kids." Then she poked what she was holding even deeper in Cat's ribs, making her wriggle.

Mrs. Grist was dangerous, and KC wanted to get her away from his friends and classmates, so he led the way. Cat followed with Bridget pressed against her to conceal what was in her hand.

They were almost out of the hall when Benjy finally noticed them leaving. "Hey Guys!" he shouted, jogging over.

"I told you to leave me alone!" KC turned and shouted, making Benjy stop short.

"Hunh?" Benjy frowned.

He had no idea that Bridget was the Stranger and that she was leading them off at gunpoint, and KC wanted to keep it that way.

"You think I'm delusional for being friends with Knox Chase?!" KC yelled to make Benjy back-off. "Well, he's a whole lot realer than your chances with Mrs. Grist. She's married, dude, so cop on and drop it!"

KC stormed off, and Benjy was about to walk away when Mrs. Bridget said, "Hold it!" just loud enough to make both of them stop.

Partially concealed by the doorway, she revealed her gun to Benjy and smiled at KC, "Nice try..."

Benjy saw the gun, but it didn't make any sense to him. He frowned and tried to explain to Mrs. Bridget, "But I like you."

It would have made KC laugh if things hadn't been so dire.

She sing-songed back, "You're very sweet, and it's a shame, but up ahead with your friend." Then she jabbed him, and he jogged beside KC.

"Sorry for the stuff I said," KC apologized.

Benjy swallowed nervously as he shook his head. "Don't worry about it."

"Turn right down that corridor," Bridget directed, and they turned down a smaller utility hallway.

They marched a few more steps before Benjy whispered, "Does the figment of your imagination have any ideas?"

KC looked at Knox hopefully, but the famous Knox Chase on the Case just said, "Keep her talking instead of shooting until something comes to you."

KC looked at Knox in disbelief, demanding "Is that the best you can do?"

Knox shrugged.

"What?" Benjy wanted to know.

"Don't get shot. That's all he's got," KC translated.

Benjy processed this and then cracked, "Not much imagination in your figment, man."

KC agreed as Knox pursed his lips and then flickered out.

Bridget warned, "That's far enough."

They stopped by a door marked "boiler/ventilation." Bridget shoved Cat over to where the boys were standing and trained her gun on them.

KC's first good look at the weapon revealed it was some kind of a semi automatic with sliding action and matted, worn black paint. A cylinder that looked like a silencer you'd see in the movies was screwed onto the end.

Bridget reached into her purse and pulled out a slender instrument made from paper clips and springs. Gun still trained on them, she jutted the thing into the keyhole and manipulated the tiny prongs by touch alone, never looking away. Then something clicked, and she pressed on the handle with the palm of her gun hand and opened the door before the kids even realized she was letting her guard down.

"Inside," she gestured to the dimly-lit stairs, leading to the basement.

The kids did as they were told, despite realizing that this woman might not be satisfied with just getting the pig.

Chapter 32

RUNNING OUT...

KC flicked a switch, and fluorescent tubes in diffusion boxes tinkled to life overhead. Their hum accompanied the kids' footsteps into the noisy basement which was almost as big as the museum's ground floor. The steps were solid pine, worn to the color of bone from decades of climbing, and the walls were painted white years ago but dust had turned them tan.

KC reached the ground first and looked around. Boilers, water pumps, furnaces, air conditioners and filtration units droned loudly along an entire wall, and shiny ventilation ducts crisscrossed the ceiling to feed air to the whole museum. Thick, filthy cellar windows loomed high up on the other side of the room, too small to escape through. There was only way out, back up the stairs.

"Over there," Bridget pointed to a steel support beam, anchored to the floor in the middle of the room.

The kids frowned at her, and she growled, "Stand around that pole!" All pretense of a smile was gone. "Now! And hold each other's hands."

She raised the gun, and the kids did what she said. KC looked at Cat, and her eyes drilled back into him that she believed everything would be okay, no matter how scared she was. He nodded that he'd take care of it.

"Owh," Benjy complained as Bridget clicked a hand-cuff around his right wrist.

KC pulled his left hand away, but she tsk-tsked and aimed her weapon at him.

He didn't realize how much he hated her until that instant, and he put his contempt into a glare as he grasped Benjy's palm again. She sneered back and chained them to one another, the handcuffs pinching KC's skin, but he wouldn't give her the satisfaction of saying anything.

"You want to talk about pain?" she needled him, working her way around to Benjy's other side and slapping another set of cuffs on his left wrist. "Pain is planning a job for 3 months, researching local losers for someone to blame it on and then getting stopped by a bunch of brats."

"Owh," Cat winced despite herself when the bracelet nicked the bone on her right wrist, locking her to Benjy.

Bridget ignored her discomfort as she walked towards Cat's other side with another pair of cuffs. "I discovered the Pagoda Pig. I uncovered Will Worth's problem past, and I made his 'bomb' out of broomsticks and an old clock," she laughed as she snapped a cuff around KC's right wrist even rougher than last time.

He gulped in pain, and Bridget grinned, "But you switched envelopes on me, and I couldn't open my mouth because Muebles would have known I wasn't Worth."

She puzzled over Cat's cast for a second before ratcheting the cuff above the plastered thumb, tight enough to chip the rock-hard gauze. Then she tugged on it, jerking Cat with the manacles. The cast wouldn't give, and Mrs. Bridget smiled at her handiwork.

She held up a flyer for the concert with a corner missing. "But I saw my opportunity with this on the bulletin board. I just had to get Ringmeyer out of the way...," she laughed, taking off her backpack now that KC, Cat and Benjy were helpless to stop her. "But I never guessed you kids would be so much trouble..."

She pulled out white surgical gloves and put them on. "I tried to take care of you last night, but you got away..."

Mrs. Bridget sauntered behind KC and plucked his cell-phone from his back pocket as Knox materialized beside him, asking "What's your plan?"

KC scoffed. His plan was to get out of this alive, only the details were hazy. They were trapped in a noisy basement with a homicidal lunatic who had already tried to kill their music teacher. Handcuffed to each other in a circle around a solid steal support beam, there was nowhere they could go.

"Not this time, though," she bubbled, yanking Benjy's phone from its hip clip.

"You think you'll get away with it?" KC challenged Bridget.

She gestured to Cat for her cellphone, but Cat just shook her head with a frown. Bridget smiled and glanced down to the bulge in her sock, beneath the folds of her long skirt.

"I know I'll get away with it," Bridget beamed.

She leaned down to the ground and retrieved Cat's cell phone from where she kept it.

"Bridget Sosaurus will so-so get away with it," she cackled, walking to the corner where she dropped the kids' cellphones and then smashed them savagely with her heel.

"Detective Grist on the other hand will leave some incriminating DNA behind when *he* steals the piggy." She danced to her backpack and pulled out a plastic baggy filled with moustache shavings. "And since they'll find you three in his hand-cuffs--".

"Find us?!" Benjy shrieked, his voice creaking as he interrupted Bridget who was tucking the baggy in her purse.

She nodded with a put-on frown, "He'll have to explain everything."

Cold raced up each of their spines, as she fished a large metal box out of her backpack and set it down just beyond the kids' reach. Custom-made from a three foot long, black toolkit with eight inch ventilation blowers welded to either side, she flicked open the shiny latches.

"This is a carbon monoxide device that blows invisible, deadly gas. I simply heat it by activating these chemical catalysts," and she started snapping open thin glass beakers.

The inert liquids inside reacted to the air, and a sinister glow ignited beneath her. She emptied the red hot contents into a ceramic bowl, closed the lid and resealed the box.

"Then I turn on these fans." They blew deafeningly despite their small size and kicked up a dust storm.

"And since this room delivers air to the entire museum," she raised her voice to be heard over the din, "in about 3 minutes every smoke alarm here will start going off. No one will know why. They'll evacuate, I'll snatch the piggy, and by the time they find you three, you won't be able to explain anything to anyone... ever again."

KC's mind raced. He knew his only chance was to conserve his breath and come up with some plan to escape, and there wasn't much time.

He wanted her to leave them already so he could get on with it, but Benjy kept her talking since he just couldn't believe it. "You're going to kill us?!"

She nodded in fake sympathy. "Ironic, too, since I don't even carry a real gun," and before they could flinch she pulled the trigger.

It doused them with water. It was a super-spray water gun in a semi automatic's frame. She pumped the slide action again and again and kept on hosing them as they tugged each other's arms while ducking the squirts.

Bridget laughed, "I put on a heck of a show don't you think?! From mild-mannered substitute to criminal mastermind." Then she whispered to KC, "And that's not *B.S.*"

KC repeated the initials, "B.S...?"

"Your dad's a big fan of my work, so I thought he'd appreciate a performance right here for his friends and family. I'm sure he'd tell me to break a leg." Bridget smiled maliciously.

"I'd tell her to take a long walk off a short pier," Knox grumbled and flickered away.

KC burned so hot with the need for revenge, he didn't even realize his friend was leaving him. He couldn't find the words to respond anyway. He just shook his head and muttered the name that had robbed him of a father all these years, *Mr. BS...*

"Time to shine," she coughed in his face from the carbon monoxide filling the room and then ran up the stairs and out the door, giggling girlishly.

Cat and Benjy screamed, "Help Us! Help Us!" But KC cut them off.

"Save your breath," he warned them. "We're going to need it."

All three of them coughed, as the air around them shimmered with deadly gas.

Chapter 33

GETTING AWAY WITH IT...?

Bridget listened to the kids shouting from the museum's ground floor service corridor. She could barely hear them in front of the closed door, and when they stopped hollering she smiled and patted down her clothing to dust herself off. Turning left to re-enter the main hall, she headed straight for the exhibition with Knox Chase right behind her.

Charlie Grist embraced her at the archway back to the Pagoda Pig room like he'd been searching for her everywhere. "Is everything okay? Can I do anything?"

She put her hands on his hips and kissed the tip of his nose, and he grinned like a dog licking his lips after a treat.

"You being you is all I need," she assured him.

A smoke alarm from the rear of the building rang with a bass, robotic note that would have shaken your teeth even if you were hard of hearing.

"What's going on?" Bridget frowned.

Another warning resounded much closer. White lights spun as a speaker in the main hall roared to life, tearing at their ear drums which they covered to protect their hearing.

"Must be a fire," Grist shouted back to her.

The kids in the hall were starting to cough, and a few of them were tearing up.

Charlie cleared his throat, "I don't smell anything, but I'm having trouble... breathing."

Bridget nodded gravely, "You've gotta get these kids out of here safely." She was already pushing him past the columns so forcefully he stumbled. "I'll make sure we don't leave anyone behind."

Grist stopped her cold and looked deep in her eyes, "This is why I love you," he choked back a sob and kissed her. Then with sockets moist and heart heavy, he hollered at nearby 6th graders, "Kids! Out. Out! OUT!"

He herded them to the entrance, and they were only too happy to evacuate with him.

"Kids... Kids!!! Anyone still here?" Bridget called with one eye on Grist making his way out the front door.

Once he was gone, she pulled a bandana out of her purse and a bottle of water which she poured into the cloth before pressing it to her mouth. Museum administrators hurried out of the building, but they appeared ready to take her with them.

She started calling for kids again and explained, "I'm with the school and have to make sure all the students get out."

They nodded and left her alone with the Pagoda Pig as the alarm kept ringing. Its metallic tones shook the building, but apart from that, the place was eerily quiet.

Bridget surveyed the room, tittering madly over how well her plan was working. Each of the four security cameras was obstructed by a ten foot tall banner she'd asked the kids to make. She danced over to the Pagoda Pig case and pulled out a ballpeen hammer. Rearing back, she plunged the sharp point into the glass and shattered it to pieces.

A new alarm buzzed in shorter, persistent bursts on top of the original warning. The noise was maddening, but all Bridget could pay attention to was the glittering Pagoda Pig right before her. Her fingers plucked it from its silken pillow, avoiding the shards of dangling glass. She tucked the statue into her purse, with the hammer on top of it, then retrieved her baggy full of Grist's mustache shavings.

"And that's why I love you, dear," she mused, dappling the broken display case with a few of her husband's hairs. Then she straightened up and reapplied her Bridget Sosaurus nice-girl expression and shouted, "All Clear!" and marched to the exit.

Knox shook his head admiringly after her, because this woman had clearly thought of everything.

Outside, on the museum steps, Bridget walked unsteadily and coughed as she said, "All clear. That's everyone."

Grist ran up and squeezed her tight. "I love you so much," he oozed affectionately.

Bridget, meanwhile, snuck a hand into her purse and pulled out her last pair of his hand-cuffs. She worked one of the bracelets onto his wrist without his even knowing. Then she spun him around while working both of his hands behind his back, and she slapped a cuff on his other wrist, too.

The loud kiss of the restraining bracelets made Grist realize what had happened, and he backed away from Bridget. "What are you doing?!"

"Detective Grist, your wife is arresting you," she teased. "Will you come quietly or do I have to get physical?"

He blushed, embarrassed to be handcuffed in front of everyone, "Very funny, but you've got to take these off now."

"Negative, prisoner. Not until you take me away from all this... on our honeymoon," she beamed, clapping.

"We can't do that," he strained against the cuffs. "What about the concert?"

"I doubt they'll even have a concert now," she shrugged and then noticed Bobby G coming up the steps towards them, and she whispered in Grist's ear, "we could even start that interrogation I promised you."

Grist giggled, but when he saw his son approaching, he shook his head.

A smile quivered on Bobby's lips as he played along, "Are you going on your honeymoon early?"

He made it sound like it was the best idea he'd ever heard, and Bridget kissed him on the cheek. "You're so sweet!-- He could go to Barb's parents' place. Couldn't you!?"

"Yeah," Bobby agreed. "It would be good for you to get a vacation, Dad. And you too..., Mom." He looked less like a bully than a scared, little kid, but he smiled on the outside even if his whole world was crumbling.

"Okay, All-right!" his Dad exclaimed, ready for a honeymoon. "If you're okay with it, my man?" Bobby nodding was all the encouragement Grist needed. "Let's do it!"

Bridget exhaled with relief as Grist turned to his son.

"Thanks, Pal! Tell Nana and Bob-Pop that I was called away a little ahead of schedule, and ask 'em to bring you to the house for the sitter around 6 o'clock. Okay?"

Knox watched helplessly, as Mrs. Bridget led Grist off to certain doom, and Bobby G nodded dumbly, his smile collapsing once they were out of view.

"Pardon me... Excuse us... Official honeymoon business," Grist announced to the kids and confused parents in front of the museum.

"But my car's at the school," he remembered, trying to call the whole thing off, until Bridget assured him that hers was on the corner.

"Your car's right here? Lucky," he told her.

"You make your own luck," she replied just as Ron Green's bureau-issued sedan pulled up to the curb in front of them.

A grin spread across Knox Chase's lips as he muttered in amazement, "Who'd have thunk it? The kid's Dad showed up..."

He'd driven all night to get there.

"Ron?" Charlie Grist exclaimed as KC's dad stepped out of the car.

"Agent Green," Bridget said, making both men look at her. She smiled broadly, "KC's told me all about you. How wonderful you could make the show, but it looks like the concert's been cancelled."

"Unh-hunh," Ron said suspiciously, glancing down at the hand-cuffs the Cornelia detective was wearing behind his back. "Well, it certainly looks like you've got your man, Miss..." He was addressing Bridget, but Grist chimed in.

"This is my new wife, Bridget Grist," Ron beamed, and Bridget snuggled closer beside him.

"Congratulations," Ron managed to contain his surprise. "To both of you."

"Thanks, we're off on our honeymoon," Grist bragged.

"This second?" Ron blurted out. "It seems like a tough time to take time off, Charlie. Don't you want to find out why the burglar alarm's ringing at the museum?"

"The fire alarm's ringing, Ron," Grist clarified.

"On top of the burglar alarm," Ron corrected him.

"I think it's just a system fault," Grist's voice wavered with doubt. Then he turned the tables. "But this isn't your jurisdiction, Special Agent. Don't you still have your hands full with the same case you've been working for years?"

"A jewel thief's had me running in circles, Charlie. I'll admit it," Ron agreed as he looked at Bridget smiling.

"Sorry to intrude, and it's so-so nice to meet you Agent Green, but we're going to be late if we don't hit the road," she apologized.

Grist nodded, but Ron didn't budge. "But weren't you supposed to be at the concert? And wasn't that scheduled to start in a half-an-hour?"

Bridget swallowed uncomfortably. "I've planned a few surprises for my groom, Mr. Green."

"Evidently," Ron smirked, "but before you go, Charlie, I'd like you to update me on the Ringmeyer case and Will Worth, and what's going on with the hit-and-run last night."

"I'm going on my honeymoon, Ron," Grist argued.

"And I'm going to figure out who tried to run my son and his friends over, Charlie, so maybe you could take off the bracelets and stay a while. While you're at it, maybe explain how Will Worth tried to hit-and-run the kids while he was in custody."

Bridget started to inch away from the two of them, but Grist turned to her.

"I was just going to bring the car around," she volunteered.

"Don't bother," he insisted, "this won't take that long."

She smiled nervously, glancing between Grist who hemmed and hawed at being second-guessed by an FBI man, and Ron Green who didn't seem to miss a thing. Except for the fact that his son and his son's friends were currently trapped inside the museum with a carbon monoxide device that would knock them all out any second.

Chapter 34

Benjy stretched to reach the bomb, but tug as he might on the cuffs, the closest he could get was still a foot from the toolbox. That was with all the kids on the tips of their toes straining around the pole. He pulled until all of their joints ached, but it was no use.

Cat suggested they use a belt to drag the device over to them, and she and KC helped Benjy get his canvas one unfastened. She swung it from her right hand, hoping to snag the handle. The belt wasn't strong enough, though, to move the toolkit. If she flicked the fabric just right she could reach the thing, but the clasp on the buckle never gripped enough to budge the box even a millimeter.

Hot air continued to shoot like jet fumes through the high-speed ventilation fans. It was a sideways plume of poison that resembled melting glass, and it made them cough and feel cloudy, like counting to three would only be possible if they could skip one and two.

KC started to see dark spots before his eyes, and Cat was wheezing from swinging the belt. She wanted to keep trying, but her coughs kept stopping her mid-fling, and then she was jerked backwards by Benjy staggering to the floor. He almost toppled both of them with him when he passed out.

"Hey, HEY!" KC prodded him, "Stay awake, Benjy. We'll get you out of here, man!"

He looked around desperately, scrambling for an idea. "Maybe we can tie our belts together," he suggested, but when he turned to Cat he found her leaning against the pole, suddenly too weak to hold herself up.

Her eyes fluttered to stay open, and she gave him the sweetest smile. "You've been amazing, KC. I really, really...," but what she really, really did, she couldn't say, because she passed out standing there, slumping against the beam.

KC shouted desperately, "We've got to stay awake, Guys!"

It was no use, though, the fumes had gotten to them. KC was starting to forget why he was still standing on his feet with those heavy weights dangling from his eyelids when Knox Chase flickered back by his side.

KC exhaled gratefully, "What do we do?!"

The detective shook his head, "You know I can't just tell you, even if I knew."

KC started to argue, but Knox cut him off, "And handcuffed to each other around a pole? You could be out of moves..."

KC swayed on his feet. "What do you--," but he was too out of breath to even finish his sentence.

He was barely able to keep his feet under him, but he knew if he leaned on the pole or sat down it would be the last thing he'd ever do, so he fought to stay awake. Meanwhile, Knox pinched his lip as his eyes swept the room for some kind of clue. They settled on Cat's cast with the tiny crack in it.

He grinned and leaned inches from KC's face to get his attention. "That BS woman sure is a cold customer. Saying '*Break A Leg...*'"

He gazed at Cat's cast, but KC couldn't shake the fog out of his head enough to grasp what he was saying, so Knox tried again, "I mean, BREAK A LEG she says, and poor Cat already has a BROKEN ARM."

Knox jerked his head at Cat's cast which was still damp from Mrs. Bridget's squirting. KC turned and finally noticed that all the straining against the hand-cuffs had made a small impression in the plaster, and the crack had gotten bigger. It was susceptible to pressure when wet.

"That's it!" KC yelled, shaking the daze out of his head. "Her arm!"

Tugging Benjy over for leeway, KC tore into the plaster. He dug his fingers into the wet wrapping, ripping out gauze and cotton around Cat's thumb. The whir of the fans disappeared in his ears as he worked the crack beneath her wrist, peeling soggy layers and snapping hard strips. Finally, he freed her fingers enough to slide the cuffs off.

"Now you're cooking, Einstein!" Knox laughed, watching KC free his right hand.

No longer trapped around the support beam, KC was still cuffed to two friends in a basement filled with deadly gas. He felt less like a genius than a zombie and couldn't think of anything to do besides screaming at his barely breathing companions.

"Guys, Guys! GUYS!!!"

He kept trying to rouse them until Knox interrupted, "KC! It's time to clear the air, don't you think?"

KC didn't understand and frowned, until Knox gestured at the high cellar window above him. *Turn off the machine. Break the window.* Got it.

KC nodded through his exhaustion and tugged Benjy by the arm so they could all move closer to the bomb. His buddy's butt made a tiny saw-dust trail in the unswept floor, before Benjy's other hand started toppling Cat off of the pole. KC rushed to her side and dragged her next to Benjy. Then he schooched both of them the last foot over to the toolbox.

He could reach it now, and KC flicked the metal latches open and nudged the top of the box with his sneaker to avoid the hot metal. He switched off the fans, and the plume of shimmering air diminished to a trickle. Then he kicked over the steel box to spill its burning hot contents onto the concrete floor. They smoked in the heavy dust, but nothing ignited, and the carbon monoxide ceased being produced. He hoped.

KC felt like lying down and going to sleep, but he knew he had to get fresh air to all of them, especially his friends. The accumulated build-up of carbon monoxide in the room could still do permanent damage or maybe even kill them.

He was a few feet below a grimy cellar window. He picked up the tool-kit with the last of his strength. He teetered beneath the weight, but thankfully, holding it by the fan edges, it wasn't hot.

Still cuffed to Benjy, KC backed up a step to get a better grip. Then he staggered towards the window and heaved the toolkit against the glass. It was the last of his everything. There wouldn't be another attempt, but the edge of the kit caught the pane perfectly, and the window shattered into three hundred pieces that dappled the floor like a crystal down-pour.

Fresh air washed over his cheeks. Their basement prison filled with blue day-light, and a ray of sunshine struck Benjy's face, making his eyes twitter and blink open.

"Benjy, Benjy!" Knox Chase called to him.

KC tried to stop him, "He can't hear you, remember?"

Knox raised an eyebrow and cracked a grin as Benjy rolled over to peer at the film noir detective who wasn't really there.

"Did you save us?" he asked. "Who are you?"

"Your pal, KC here, did the heavy lifting. I was mostly moral support," Knox confided, leaning down. "Speaking of moral support, why don'cha go a little easier with the figment talk, okay?" He jammed his thumbs into his chest, "Since this figment is a little sensitive."

Benjy was still coming out of his daze when he realized that Knox was black and white AND semi-transparent, "What! How come... Who are you?"

"I'm Knox Chase. On the Case," he told Benjy, who was utterly speechless. Then Knox turned back to KC. "I told you I could take care of him for you."

KC shook his head, laughing, as Knox hollered, "And don't forget the canoodling pig-pincher trying to get away."

Then Knox flickered off, leaving Benjy shaking his head. "How'd he do that?" he spluttered.

"Who? Do what?" KC responded, and then he smiled knowingly at Benjy who scrambled to his feet, giggling and nervous to be in on the secret.

Cat moaned, coming around, and KC knelt beside her.

"Cat, Cat! Wake up, Cat..." KC shook her shoulders gently.

She squinted then smiled dreamily, muttering,"...I like you..."

Then she opened her eyes and looked at KC and blushed, but KC smiled back at her, and she sat up.

Glancing around the room at the broken window and the disabled device and her own mushy cast, she asked "What happened? I thought..."

KC grinned and helped her to her feet. "I told you I'd get you out of this--"

Still a little shaky, she gripped him tightly, trembling.

They hugged until KC pulled away and grinned, "Now let's go crash a honeymoon."

Chapter 35

Knox Chase flickered into being in front of the museum as Mary Green ran up the block beside an older man in a dress police uniform. Her hair flew in loose strands, and she was panting since she'd started running from her house as soon as she heard the alarms blaring across town. Cornelia Police Chief Williamson, the man in the uniform, had only joined her for the last hundred feet or so, but both of them arrived in a huff beside Ron Green.

The Chief furrowed his brows in disbelief at Grist, whose hands were still cuffed behind him. "Charlie?"

"Sorry, sir," Grist apologized, "Just kidding. My new wife and I were just... just having a joke on our way to our honeymoon. Do you want to uncuff me, honey?" Grist asked Bridget, but she fumbled about in her purse like she couldn't find the key.

Chief Williamson shook his head in disgust. Meanwhile, Mary came over and kissed Ron on the cheek.

"I didn't really believe it last night when you said that you'd be here." Then she searched the crowd for the kids. "Where's KC?"

"I thought he was with you," Ron started, scanning the steps of the museum and the faces in the crowd.

KC and his friends were nowhere to be seen.

"Don't worry," Charlie assured them, "Bridget made sure everyone got out, didn't you, sweetie?" He reached for his new wife, but she was six feet closer to her car, tiptoeing away when everyone turned and looked at her.

She froze like a cat in the head-lights, a guilty smile playing across her lips. Then the fire alarm stopped ringing in the museum, leaving just the burglar alarm. Bridget's eyes went wide, and she pulled her purse a little closer.

"Honey," Charlie asked, "Could you unfasten my cuffs now?"

She nodded then pulled out the ballpeen hammer and leapt behind Grist. Kicking his legs out from under him, he fell to his knees, and she pressed the sharp point against his temple.

"Hands up, or I splatter tiny brains all over you," Bridget screamed.

"What the heck is going on here, Charlie?" Chief Williamson demanded, but Grist ignored him as he looked up at his bride.

"You were just using me?" he begged her to disagree.

"Brilliant deduction. Now! Nobody moves while we get in my car," Bridget hissed.

"But what about the kids?" Mary shouted, taking a step closer.

Ron grabbed Mary's arm to stop her and said to Mrs. Grist, "Take me, Mr. BS. That is who you are, right?" Bridget smiled slyly as he went on. "You always find a patsy to pin your crimes on. This time you picked a perp in my own town to embarrass me. Smart."

Bridget grinned back at him, and Ron turned to his wife, "You go in and get the kids. I'll take care of this."

Mary looked in his eyes, making sure he understood that this woman would kill him if he let her. Ron understood.

Bridget shouted, "Nobody move!"

Ron repeated to his wife, "Just get the kids."

Mary looked at him again, biting her lip, then she nodded and dashed towards the entrance as Bobby G ran up shouting, "Dad!"

Grist looked desperately at his son pleading, "Stay there! Don't come any closer."

Bobby stopped short and cried, "Let him go! Now!"

Bridget scrunched up her face and shrugged like it was out of her control.

Ron walked over to her slowly, his hands in the air. "Bridget Grist, or whoever you are, I'm the one you want. You keep me, and the investigation is over. Nobody else has to get hurt."

Charlie Grist's eyes went wide, and they darted from Ron to Bobby and back up to Bridget, who was thinking this offer over. She smiled, like the idea of rubbing out Ron Green was delicious, but she started to shake her head when Mary hollered from the base of the museum's front steps.

"The Kids!"

All heads turned where she was pointing to see the three of them trudging down the steps in single file. Cat in the lead and KC bringing up the rear, still hand-cuffed, coated in grime and squinting in the daylight.

He raised his free hand to shield his eyes and saw his dad standing across from Bridget. "It's Mr. BS, Dad," he shouted. "She did it! Bridget Sosaurus!"

KC ran over to them, dragging Benjy and Cat behind him. They flapped like kite ribbons in a big wind as he snaked his way through the crowd.

Ron's gaze never wavered from Mrs. Bridget as he replied. "Thanks, KC, I'll take it from here."

His hands up in front of her with Grist shaking his head miserably at her feet, Ron tried reassuring Mrs. Bridget, "You don't have to hurt him."

The entire town gathered around to watch them, and a fire engine rumbled up to block them in. No one moved or even dared to breathe too loudly, as she started backing away towards the ladder truck, her eyes darting side to side. Grist was shuffling on his knees, trying to keep up, and she wasn't getting very far.

"With or without that moustache, you're the worst detective I've ever met, Charlie. Now get up!" she snarled.

"Leave him alone!" Bobby G broke down screaming.

"I don't want to go...," Charlie begged.

He was sniffling, teary-eyed, glancing around pleading for someone to do something as the kids emerged at the front of the crowd. Bridget inched closer to KC, and he slowly reached his hand into the top of his backpack for the eye-piece of his monoscope.

"There's nowhere left to go and nothing you can do, Bridget," his dad told their substitute.

"I wouldn't say that," she sneered, raising the hammer, ready to bash Grist's temple in.

Whether Mrs. Bridget was bluffing, no one knew. Grist flinched and looked away. Ron Green reached for something behind his back, but KC was quicker.

"Not so fast!" He hollered, and Mrs. Bridget looked up at him as he yanked the monoscope out of his backpack and unfurled it directly into her face.

It telescoped open, and the big lens smashed her between the eyes with a pop that split the thick glass in two. She stood there, not quite falling and not quite standing, just swaying in an invisible breeze. Dazed, she let the hammer slip out of her hand, and it hit the ground.

She might have stayed like that indefinitely, but Mr. Jenkins appeared from behind the fire truck, swinging his walking stick like a baseball bat. The rubber handle collided with the back of her head, and Bridget Sosaurus Grist, or whatever her name was, crumpled to her knees and splatted flat against the asphalt, unconscious.

"That's for leaving my apartment in a state!" Mr. Jenkins declared, as Special Agent Green rushed over to where she lay and slapped hand-cuffs on her wrists at the small of her back.

Then he looked up at KC, who was holding his mangled monoscope in front of him, mouth open and astonished at what he'd done.

"Are you crazy?!" Ron Green shouted at his son, and KC blinked. "She could have seriously hurt you...," Ron stepped over Bridget and hugged KC tightly, dragging Benjy and Cat along with him, not that they minded.

He would never have let go, except a rough hand spun him around and made him drop KC.

It belonged to Mary Green who insisted "Him? What about you?!"

She shook her husband hard by both shoulders, and then she pulled his face towards hers and kissed him. Deeply. With tears in her eyes.

KC laughed, overwhelmed by his mom and dad seemingly back together. Benjy and Cat patted him on the back to congratulate him.

Bobby G even came over. He was pale and still shaking, and he swallowed a couple of times before opening his mouth, making KC think barf might come out.

Instead, Bobby whispered, "Thanks for saving my, Dad."

Before KC could respond, Bobby G looked down and walked over to where Charlie Grist still knelt on the ground, and hugged him for all he was worth. *At least Bobby didn't punch me in the stomach again*, KC thought.

Mary Green came up for air and said, "I don't want to let you go, bud."

She held Ron tremblingly close, her head resting on his chest until Chief Williamson walked up and cleared his throat.

KC's parents broke apart, and Ron looked at the Chief who announced "I don't know if you're aware of it, but I'll be stepping down as head of the department in a few weeks, and the search for my replacement is suddenly wide open."

Both of them glanced at Grist. Hands still cuffed behind his back and his son hugging him, his head drooped looking over at his soon to be ex-wife.

Ron rubbed his chin, interested.

"Just think about it," the Chief continued, "and let me take care of those cuffs."

The kids were still chained together, and Grist sighed as he eyed the Chief unfastening them.

Williamson thanked Cat, KC and Benjy for their bravery, as KC explained, "She's got the Pagoda Pig in her purse."

Ron pulled the statue out of the bag and held it up proudly as a reporter for the Cornelia paper snapped a quick shot.

KC went on, "She wrote the ransom note, ran over our chorus teacher and tried to rob the museum, oh and she was our substitute music teacher."

"And she didn't know a thing about music," Cat concluded like that was her greatest offense.

Hearing her exploits recounted made Bridget lift her chin blearily off the asphalt.

Benjy leaned down beside her. "You really hurt my feelings. We could have had something," he confided.

She groaned, and her head fell back onto the road.

Meanwhile, Grist looked up meekly at Williamson. "Chief? My cuffs?"

He walked over with keys in hand. "I'm sorry Charlie, did you want to run your wife in or should I?"

Everyone laughed. Even Bobby G chuckled through his sniffles.

Knox started to walk towards KC, but seeing him with his friends and family, he must have thought better of it, because instead he just flickered away, grinning.

Chapter 36

FAREWELL... FOR NOW

The concert was cancelled that day, but five weeks later the sixth grade class of Roosevelt Elementary School was finally able to sing their tribute to the Amazing Asia Exhibit. The whole town turned out, not only to congratulate the kids who'd single-handedly saved the collection's masterpiece, but also to see their new Chief of Police in action.

Mr. Ringmeyer conducted the show in leg braces and on crutches, and the kids assembled around the Pagoda Pig to blast their ten-minute Mikado mash-up. Cat had no fewer than five solos, and each one earned a standing ovation.

When the singing concluded, KC and Benjy hustled down the risers to take their place beside her in the circle of honor. With some nudging from Mary Green in the audience, Will was persuaded to join them. Then KC's dad walked up to the podium in his Cornelia Chief of Police uniform, and Knox Chase materialized between KC and Benjy.

Knox joked, "Is this the part where you tell everyone you couldn't have done it without me?"

"It's a little annoying having your very own figment isn't it?" Benjy remarked.

KC nodded with a broad smile on his face, and Cat ssshhh'd them.

Ron Green grinned, then cleared his throat to begin, "There are all kinds of heroes. There's the person who makes a mistake and has the courage to make it right." He looked over at Will in his suit and tie who mouthed the words 'thank you.'

"There are the brave few who fight for the truth, no matter who or what stand in their way," Chief Green continued, looking at the kids who beamed back at him.

"There's the strong, silent type who doesn't need acknowledgement... evidently," Knox groused, making Benjy and KC crack up a little.

Ron Green looked straight at his son. "And there are folks who sacrifice for family and friends in the hope that they can make the world what it could be. Every day. My son taught me what it takes to be this kind of hero. KC, I love you."

"I love you too, Chief!" KC called back to him, as Mary wiped away a tear.

Chief Green smiled wide until he remembered he wasn't done, "So, without further ado, I award each of you this Commendation for Valorous Service..." He looked for his reluctant deputy to hand out the medals, and Charlie Grist frowned and stood up in a regular patrolman's uniform with four long velvet cases in his hands.

Grist walked up to Will first, opened a box and scowlingly hung a medal around the ex-convict's neck.

"Thank you, officer," Will said with a straight face.

Grist smirked and then just thrust cases into KC, Cat and Benjy's hands while Chief Green declared, "... in humble acknowledgement of your actions, the people of Cornelia owe you a debt of gratitude."

The auditorium rose to its feet and applauded and continued applauding with whoops and cheers for the kids who'd saved the day and the innocent man who'd defended them. The four heroes choked up a little as they waved and smiled, but Knox Chase just scratched his head.

He sauntered over between KC and Cat and whispered, "Here's where you hold her hand, partner."

KC didn't quite hear him, and he repeated, "Hold her hand?"

Cat turned to him, blushing, and she said "Okay," and held out her hand for him to take.

He took a breath and then clasped her palm in his. It felt hot and soft and wonderful. He squeezed, and she squeezed back, and now they were both red-faced and smiling wide, and he'd done it. He and Cat were maybe, possibly, it-could-be even more than friends. Maybe.

Cheeks on fire and his heart bursting out of his chest, KC would have gone on holding her hand for hours, but the crowd of Cornelia citizens was closing in to congratulate their heroes, and Knox started heading for the open auditorium door.

He called to KC and Benjy over his shoulder as he walked out, "I'll see you in the funny pages, Partners."

Benjy and KC grinned at one another and then looked back at Knox as he was flickering in the distance.

"But you'll always know where to find me. Just look on page 1," the detective called after them as clapping townspeople blocked their view for an instant. When they parted, he was gone.

KC wasn't worried, though. He knew he could count on Knox if trouble ever came back to town.

Cat and Benjy and KC hugged. Will shook hands with Ron Green, and then his wife emerged from the crowd with a determined expression on her face, and this time she didn't have to shake her husband before she kissed him.

All the while, the Pagoda Pig sparkled safely on its pillow. On its plinth. Beneath glass. Because Knox Chase had friends who were with him on the Case.

Acknowledgements

I've worked on this book for over seven years and have badgered legions into helping me. Without them, Knox Chase would be a gimmicky shadow of the full-fledged shadow he's become. KC would annoy you with his falsely ingratiating antics, and all the other characters in this story would probably tick you off, too.

If some or all of the above remains to be the case, please don't hold it against any of the following readers, because my wife insists that I don't listen, so it isn't their fault: Danielle Appel, Chris Olsen, Caleb and Tehilla Fishman, Gail Axt, Carole Quimby, Sophia Wright, Gabby Lessans, Oliver and Joel Brenner, Rebecca and David Shaff, Laine Armstrong, Stefanie Jones (my high school prom date), Will Mortell, Michael Potts, Max Straub, Alaine Janosy, Ann Goldensohn (my sixth grade teacher), Paula Lipsius, Steven Lipsius, Dorothy Lipsius, Eli Lipsius, Elizabeth Lipsius (miraculously, none of whom is any relation to me). Every single one of these people dedicated their time and insight into making this a much better story, and I can never repay them. Or at least it would cost more than I'm willing to spend.

All of the young actors who brought versions of this story to life out-loud in the Uptown 6 Youth Lab over the Fall of 2014 (Jillian, Vince, Cole, Garrett, Dirkson, Sarai, Peter, Maya, Darr, Sam, Ella, Kylee, Leah, Kyleigh, Amelia, Alec and Danny), you let me live the characters vicariously through your eyes, and I'm grateful.

Brigid Pasulka, the most amazing author ever born, actually line edited the entire book while simultaneously writing her own book and delivering a child. Seriously. I can't talk on the telephone if the tv is on, and she did all of that because she's that good.

Ian Henson, my fearless friend, suffered through multiple drafts while juggling production responsibilities in my office. Ransom Riggs (my old film school producing partner), his wife Tahereh Mafi, Amy (Lipsius) Halpern (also no relation), Sean Covel and Hal Sadoff all provided invaluable support, making me think this might actually happen.

My agent, Alex Slater at Trident kept pushing me and pushing me and... you get the idea, until this thing read like soup through a fork, and finally Linda Lipsius, who bears a striking resemblance to my wife and has believed in me and this book far longer than a sensible person would have is the only reason I'm not face down in a gutter. But I'm still not going to say it.

So, thank you to everyone!

Who the Heck Wrote This?

Born in 1972, Adam Lipsius was bound and determined to be a kid for as long as possible, and so far so good. The director and producer of a movie called *16-LOVE*, Linda's husband and Dorothy & Eli's Dad, he walks the streets of Denver concocting stories out of pure fantasy. Sometimes he drinks coffee and eats oatmeal, but when inspiration attacks, he lives on hope alone. Hope and Pringles and Teatulia Tea.

This is his first book-book, though, he did write a critical biography of Dr. Seuss when he was in college called <u>The Birth of Dr. Seuss.</u>

If you want Knox Chase back on the Case again soon, tell your friends about his story, today!